THE A-TEAM IV:
OLD SCORES TO SETTLE

The gunman held himself back from striking his captive again, although his face was flushed with rage. He grabbed a roll of packing tape, fuming.

But before the adhesive could be applied to the luckless chef's mouth, a rattle of gunfire echoed through the room, and the area around Lin the chef and his abductors began to look like a shooting gallery in full swing as bullets ripped into the walls and skimmed across the floor.

Hannibal and BA followed their barrage into the room, then let their guns go silent.

'Okay boys,' Hannibal advised the culprits. 'Down with your guns and up with your hands!'

'You guys!' the limo driver cried, recognising Hannibal and BA from the restaurant. 'Couldn't stay away, could you?'

Hannibal shook his head. 'You ran off with the chef before we could give him our compliments. Bad etiquette. We'll have to teach you some manners . . .'

THE A-TEAM IV:
OLD SCORES TO SETTLE

A novel by Charles Heath

Based on the television series 'The A-Team'
Created by Frank Lupo and Stephen J. Cannell
Adapted from the episodes 'The Only Church in Town'
written by Babs Greyhosky, and 'Recipe for Heavy Bread'
written by Stephen J. Cannell.

TARGET

published by
the Paperback Division of
W. H. ALLEN & Co. PLC

A Target Book
Published in 1984
by the Paperback Division of
W.H. Allen & Co. PLC
44 Hill Street, London W1X 8LB

Printed and bound in Great Britain by
Anchor Brendon Ltd, Tiptree, Essex

ISBN 0 426 19828 X

ONE

People don't *eat* lunch in Hollywood; they *do* it. In fact, the phrase 'let's do lunch' is the most often used in the divine trilogy of pat sayings that constitute the primary conversational arsenal of most moguls in the land of tinsel, followed by 'let's take a meeting' and '*ciao!*' Pronounced 'chow', '*ciao*' is not part of Hollywoodese, since, after all, 'doing chow' falls drearily short of conjuring up the proper image of glamorous, tax-break dining on sushi, escargot, or whatever other buzzfood happens to enthral the chic, communal appetite of the industry's prime movers during any given season. What one eats, however, is not nearly as important as where one eats, in this town. There are many prestigious eating places that cater to the showbiz elite and operate with an air of snobbish exclusivity that would make most country clubs seem like fast-food joints in comparison, but there is no establishment more desirable for the ego-starved than Arkan's, a posh dining lounge located a quick chauffeur-drive from three major studios. Steeped in tradition and pretention, Arkan's is decorated in elegant brocade and polished teak, and staffed by preening Frenchmen who spend as much time cultivating their native accents as they do their prim little moustaches.

All things considered, Arkan's seemed to be a rather unlikely choice for lunch by the likes of the A-Team, and yet, as the noon rush was in full swing, an unmistakable black van with diagonal crimson striping pulled off Sunset Boulevard and double-parked adjacent to one of many sleek, gleaming limousines hugging the curve in front of the prestigious restaurant. A crew of red-jacketed valets eyed the vehicle as if it were a UFO that had just swooped down from the planetary heavens, and, after a brief huddle, the attendant with the least seniority was dispatched to see if those inside the van had perhaps just lost their way or were looking for maps to the homes of the stars. Before he could reach the van, the passenger's door swung open and Templeton Peck stepped out, wearing a cream-coloured Calvin Klein suit with matching silk shirt and the kind of engaging smile used-car salesmen spend their whole lives trying to master.

'What say, André?' Peck greeted the valet as he moved over to open the side door of the van. 'The Lincoln's in the shop for the day. This was the only loaner they had. Belongs to the mechanic.'

'Oh ... yes, yes, of course,' André stammered, stepping to one side as the three passengers in the back of the van emerged. Hannibal Smith snugly filled out a conservative navy-blue suit, looking like a banker out to celebrate a clean audit. Amy Allen wore a bone-white dress that hung a good five inches above her knees, exposing a pair of slim, tanned legs that tucked nicely into calf-high leather boots. The lump in André's throat ducked for cover behind his bow-tie as he swallowed hard and tried to wrench his gaze from Amy. As if to aid the valet in his plight, Howling Mad Murdock brought up the rear, springing out of the van with a gangly aloofness. Murdock's lone concession to Arkan's recommended dress code was the imprint of a tuxedo stamped onto the t-shirt he wore under his flight jacket, although he had also made a point of wearing his cleanest baseball cap and sneakers.

'Cast members from my new film,' Peck informed André as he gestured to his associates. 'We rushed over from a shoot, so they didn't have time to change.'

'I see.' André smiled thinly as the entourage strolled past him and went on to engage the disbelieving stares of the other valets, then circled around to the driver's side of the van and opened the door.

'Good day, sir, may I ...'

André's voice trailed off and his Adam's apple geared up

6

for another game of hide-and-seek as he stared at BA, Baracus, who loomed behind the steering wheel in his usual attire of gold chains and jewellery, cut-off slacks and vest, and sculpted Mandinka haircut.

'May you what, sucker?' BA demanded, glowering at André

'Uh... your car... I mean van... vehicle... may I park your vehicle?'

'No way!' BA retorted, grinding gears. 'Nobody drives my wheels but me, man!'

As BA screeched rubber and raced off to a parking spot down the block, André wandered numbly back to the kerb, where the rest of the A-Team lingered, waiting for their associate. Hannibal noted the valet's consternation and assured him, 'Mr Baracus is a famous French actor. A little eccentric, but a talent with no equal.'

The others nodded their affirmation, but André wasn't convinced. 'He didn't look French. And his accent, well...'

'Now, now, André,' Peck chided, 'You have to realize he studied at the Harvard School of Performing Arts for five years. He's mastered no less than a dozen dialects.'

'He knows lots of ways to talk, too,' Murdock said.

André looked down the block as BA got out of the van and headed back to the restaurant. 'But, I'm afraid he's parked in a temporary loading zone. There's a stiff –'

'Don't move that van, sucker,' BA threatened, prodding André's sternum with one of his many-ringed fingers, 'or I'll come out here and feed you your socks!'

As BA and the others headed off down the carpeted walkway leading into Arkan's, Murdock applauded, closing his eyes like someone in the throes of spectatorial ecstacy. 'Encore! Encore!'

'Sir?' André said, still trembling visibly from BA's warning.

Murdock opened his eyes and looked at André as if he were an unenlightened heathen, then gushed, 'Why, don't you know when you've just been treated to a free glimpse of genius in action?'

'What?'

7

'The famous "Feed You Your Socks" speech from *Right on, Ruth*, the Pulitzer Prize-winning play by Margaret Hanley. Surely you're familiar with it. He delivered it beautifully, don't you think? Just the perfect blend of tragic hauteur...'

'Murdock!' Hannibal called out from the entrance to the restaurant. 'Save some of it for dinner conversation, all right?'

'Coming.' Before leaving André, though, Murdock squeezed the valet's arm and whispered, 'Just remember, you have been truly honoured...'

As Murdock wandered off, André glanced over at his fellow attendant and shrugged his shoulders, muttering, 'Crazy Americans. Anything to avoid tipping...'

In sharp contrast to the bright, airy exterior of Arkan's, the dining area within was cloaked in a cavern-like darkness. Devoid of functional windows, any trace of the outside sunlight was blocked from view, and the few dim lamps suspended from the ceiling threw more illumination on the framed photographs of dead celebrities on the walls than on the tables where the living came to dine at the mercy of candlelight. The atmosphere was decidedly meant to invoke a sense of shrouded intimacy, and yet few of the diners frequented Arkan's to share an intimate meal. The majority of customers spent only a small portion of their time engaging in conversation with their dining companions; their gazes invariably drifted from their tables to take in the activities around them. Tabloid writers and other gossip-mongers nursed drinks as they kept their senses attuned to pick up the latest dirt or a whiff of next week's big trend around town. Agents were on the lookout for producers or executives they could collar with pitches on behalf of unseen clients, and a scattering of stars lounged about, loving the attention cast their way and forever shifting their faces to provide onlookers with glimpses of their favourite profiles.

The arrival of the A-Team cut a sudden swath of silence through the restaurant, and those seated beat their brains feverishly, trying to decide if they should know this strange fivesome that had suddenly intruded upon their presence.

8

Whispered speculation had the new arrivals pegged as everything from a contingent of East Coast investors to the cast of a new musical opening at the Pantages to the industry's underground suppliers of recreational stimulants. The A-Team stopped short of entering the dining room and waited by the cashier's desk for service, basking in their instant notoriety. The head waiter spotted them from across the room and started over in a huff, sticking his chin out and his nose up further with each step as he fidgeted with the lapels of his tuxedo.

'Sucker's gonna tell us to go to Burger King,' BA grumbled.

'Now, BA, I already told you we'd get the red carpet treatment here,' Peck calmed him. 'Trust me.'

'Last time I trusted you I got shot in the leg,' BA reminded Peck.

The head waiter seemed ready to deliver a farewell address when he picked out Peck's face in the group. His jutting chin lowered immediately, making way for a warm smile as he stepped forward and offered Peck a mild but enthusiastic embrace.

'Ah, Mr Peck,' he warbled. 'How marvellous to see you again. Your table is waiting for you.'

'How sweet of you, Henri,' Peck beamed. 'No doubt about it, you run the best restaurant in the city.'

'We try, monsieur,' Henri said with a smile as he plucked up a handful of menus from the stand beside him. 'Have you ever been to our Sunday brunch before? We have a finely-prepared buffet, not to mention a wide selection –'

'How long's this jive goin' on before we get any food, man?' BA interrupted, crossing his arms. 'We came here to *eat*.'

Henri's smile curdled and he blinked his eyes as if he hoped BA was an illusion caused by a blur on his contacts. Retaining his poise, he motioned to the dining room. 'Allow me to take you to your table.'

As the group waded into the luxurious surroundings, the stares cast their way intensified, with Murdock and BA drawing the most attention. Murdock removed his cap in a gesture of appeasement, but BA scowled at the onlookers with unchecked defiance. Under his breath he muttered to Amy, 'I ain't seen this many turkeys since Thanksgiving!'

'Easy, BA,' Face said. 'You'll like the food and it'll all be worthwhile.'

'I don't eat nothin' I can't pronounce,' BA warned.

There was only one vacant table in the whole restaurant, located under a multi-tiered chandelier in the middle of the dining room. Henri pulled out a chair for Amy while the men seated themselves.

'I have ordered a bottle of Mr Peck's favourite wine for your table,' Henri told the group. 'Our compliments. Enjoy, enjoy.'

'Merci,' Peck said, placing a hand on the head waiter's arm. 'You are a treasure, Henri.'

Henri offered the group a diffident bow, then ambled off to begin calming the patrons who seemed the most distressed over the invasion of their select ranks by undesirables like Murdock and BA.

'When's the wedding, Face?' Hannibal asked Peck as he snapped open his napkin and laid it across his lap. 'Or have you and Henri already eloped?'

'Head waiters need to be stroked, Hannibal,' Peck defended himself. 'And BA, just keep it buttoned, will ya? It's bad enough you looking like an extra from "Fort Apache" without giving Henry a bad time. Look, I've already run three film scams outta here, so don't go killing my golden goose, all right?'

'Goose, hmmmm.' Murdock opened his menu and skimmed through the entrees. 'Goose, what a splendid idea. I'd just love to take a gander, glazed with a subtle orange sauce, resting on a bed of crisp parsley... aw, drat, the closest they have here is duck. Duck won't do when you've got a mind for goose.'

'You've got a mind for rent, fool,' BA taunted.

Murdock stuck his tongue out at BA while Peck offered apologetic smiles to the diners at the tables around them. Hannibal perused the appetizers and Amy glanced over at the far wall, where a handful of chefs dressed in white toiled over a buffet table, arranging food with careful precision of interior decorators. 'Okay, Face,' she asked, 'which one is he?'

As the others looked the chefs over, BA grunted, 'He ain't here, man.'

'He's probably in the supply room,' Face said. 'I know it's him, it's gotta be. At first I thought I was wrong, but the more I ate here... especially the bread... Remember that bread he used to cook? The hint of ginseng? Remember that?'

There was a basket on the table containing a loaf of fresh bread wrapped in a burgundy napkin. When Hannibal uncovered it, the aroma wafted out in all directions, earning a pleasurable hum from Amy and Murdock. Hannibal broke off a large piece of the bread and passed it around. As they all sampled the offering, another waiter arrived with the wine and poured a few drops into Peck's glass. Grasping the stem, Peck raised the glass and inspected the clarity of the wine in the lights of the chandelier, then slowly sipped the contents before pronouncing, 'Dry and light and magnificent, as always. Thanks.'

The waiter began filling the other glasses as BA chewed down his share of the bread. 'Man,' he said between chomps, 'this tastes just like the bread we got in our Viet Cong prison camp.'

Overhearing the remark, the waiter stopped pouring wine and stood upright, bristling at the imagined insult. Peck stretched his leg under the table and kicked BA in the shins to silence him. Murdock dabbed his lips with his napkin and adlibbed, with effete smugness, 'You must realize, darling, the cuisine in North Vietnamese prison camps was highly underrated. The sauces were exquisite. The brown gravy was simmered in wine. We all got fat on Zsa Zsa's poodles.'

The waiter blanched at the comparison, but summoned enough composure to finish pouring the wine.

'They're comedians from the Second City opening at the Comedy Store,' Peck explained to the waiter. 'A riot, aren't they? It's so hard to get them out of character, though.'

'Of course, sir.' The waiter rolled his eyes as he set the half-

11

emptied bottle in an ice bucket next to the table. As he walked off, Peck stared harshly at BA and Murdock.

'Come on, you guys. Will you try and not burn this place for me?'

After Amy finished nibbling her piece of the bread, she said, 'Face, you can't really think that the cook at your POW camp ten years ago is the pastry chef in this restaurant.'

'Amy's right,' Hannibal put in. 'I'l grant you, this bread tastes mighty familiar, but it just doesn't add up. I mean, how could Lin Duck Coo have gotten out of Communist territory in one piece?'

'Who knows?' Peck said. 'Maybe the same way we did.'

'We really owe that little guy,' Murdock explained to Amy.

'How so?'

'They had a general in that camp with a mean streak a mile wide,' Murdock said. 'His idea of a good time was starving prisoners. We had guys dying from malnutrition. Lin Duk Coo used to sneak us food. He kept a lot of grunts alive, and he risked his life doing it. If General Kao had caught him, he would've killed him, no question about it.'

'Sounds like quite a man,' Amy reflected. 'Maybe Face is right then. If he could have sneaked food to you, maybe he could have sneaked himself to freedom, don't you think?'

'Anything's possible,' Hannibal conceded.

'Man, this bread tastes like his, all right,' BA said, grabbing another piece from the loaf.

Just then the doors to the kitchen swung open and a diminutive figure pushed out a tray filled with pastries. He had a chef's hat pulled down around his head, but enough of his features were visible to reveal his eastern heritage. Without spotting the A-Team, the chef rolled his cart to the buffet and joined his fellow cooks in arranging the table.

'There,' Face whispered, drawing the others' attention to the buffet. 'There, now is that Lin Duk Coo, or is that his twin brother, or what?'

'Son of a gun,' Hannibal muttered, staring across the room. 'Sure as hell looks like him.'

'We gotta find out for sure,' Murdock said.

'Why not just ask him?' Amy suggested. 'Face, why didn't you just get his attention when you first thought it was him anyway? I don't get it.'

'Well, I was kinda hesitant to say anything then,' Face said. 'I mean, I was supposed to be an Ivy League producer and I was here with other people... you know, bigwig types. It just didn't seem appropriate to stand up in a fancy place like this and call out his name...'

Rising from his chair, BA cupped his hands around his mouth and shouted across the room, 'Hey, Lin Duk Coo!'

TWO

Lin Duk Coo had come to work at Arkan's under the name of Peter Pereime, and as far as anyone at the restaurant was concerned, he was not a Vietnamese refugee and secret saviour of American POWs, but rather the long-time adopted son of a native California family currently living in Orange County. He had kept his true origins secret for good reason, and the moment he heard someone call out his name in the dining room, his instincts had conspired with his adrenalin to determine a course of action – immediate flight. From his experience, he assumed that the only people in Los Angeles who knew of him from the days of the war were people whose overwhelming preference was to see him dead. As such, without wasting precious seconds to see who it was that had called his name, Lin bolted for the nearest exit.

'Ay-yi-yi!' he howled, overturning his pastry cart and jarring the buffet table enough to topple the intricately stacked offerings of food in his haste to rush through the swinging doors that led to the kitchen.

'Hey, Lin, it's me, BA, Baracus!' BA shouted, rushing off in pursuit of the fleeing chef. Rather than negotiate around the bulky planter separating a row of booths in the centre of the room, BA hurdled the obstacle, crashing through the fronds of a thick fern and almost landing in the lap of an elderly woman who sat trembling at her booth.

'Please don't hurt me!' the woman pleaded, 'I'm going to be a grandmother!'

'I'll write you a cheque,' her husband offered.

'Man, just get outta my way!' BA snapped, unsnagging himself from the tablecloth and trying to push past the

14

bewildered patrons.

Gasps and cries rang out from the other tables as diners sprang from their chairs, contemplating flight from what they assumed to be an outburst of escalating violence that was the inevitable consequence of letting commoners in off the streets and within smelling range of wealth and sophistication. The pandemonium spread like choice gossip, providing adequate diversion for the rest of the A-Team to abandon their table and try to elbow their way out the way they'd come. Halfway to the front door, Face found himself nose to nose with the head waiter, whose amiable demeanour had vanished under the burden of shock and indignation.

'Thank you so much, Henri,' Face cooed breathlessly as he hurried by with Hannibal, Murdock, and Amy. 'Hate to run, but, as always, your hospitality has been . . .' Face could only kiss the tips of his fingers to approximate the depth of his feelings about the accommodations. Hannibal dragged him away before he could offer a tip to back his desperate flattery.

As the A-Team was heading for the front exit, Lin entered the kitchen well ahead of BA, barrelling headlong into the head chef, a potbellied Swede who was carrying an armload of clean pots back to the grill.

'Vot der hell . . .'

Reeling backwards from the force of impact, the cook slipped on a puddle of water spilled from the dishwashing machine. He flailed his arms wildly in a last-ditch effort to regain his balance, but succeeded only in dropping the pans and falling backwards into a dishrack, upsetting that as well. His steady flow of Scandinavian obscenities was muffled by the din of clanging pots and shattering china. Lin was also knocked off balance by the collision and deflected into the side of a counter where a tubful of fresh lobsters was soaking in cold water. The crustaceans were given a brief stay of execution as Lin overturned their tub in his haste to keep up his forward momentum and follow the quickest route to the back exit. By the time BA had rushed into the kitchen, Lin was out the door, leaving behind an obstacle course of fallen cooking utensils, china shrapnel, scuttling lobsters, and a half-crazed Swedish chef who looked like someone trying out for Ingmar Bergman's first venture into slapstick comedy.

If the restaurant was the figurative frying pan Lin Duk Coo was jumping from, the back parking lot was the proverbial fire. A long, black limousine had just rolled into the lot, and climbing out of the vehicle were two of Lin's true adversaries, a pair of men with rugged features and brute physiques crammed into Brooks brothers suits. The one in the blue suit was toting an Israeli Uzi submachine gun, and as Lin headed for his rundown Chevy Nova, a chorus line of hot lead danced in front of him, forcing him to stop in his tracks.

'Where you think you're goin', egg roll?' the gunman shouted. 'Freeze!'

As the gunman took a step towards Lin, BA raced out the back way, converging with the rest of the A-Team, which had circled around from the front of the restaurant. Before any of them could properly assess the situation and take appropriate action, a volley of gunfire ripped through the air above their heads.

'Everybody on the ground!' the man with the Uzi barked. 'Now, or you all get polka dots!'

The A-Team hugged the asphalt, looking like a group of civilians preparing to do push-ups during lunch hour on orders from the company fitness advisor.

'I hate polka dots,' Face moaned quietly. 'Especially red ones.'

'This is what I get for dressing up on account of your geek friends,' Hannibal said to Face. 'You owe me a new suit.'

'From the look of things, I guess you might get fit for it at the mortuary,' Face replied, staring at the submachine gun pointed their way. 'He touches that trigger and we're ground round.'

But the man with the Uzi was more interested in Lin Duk Coo than the A-Team. He stalked over to where the chef had dived to the pavement, while his partner got back into the limo and pulled up in front of the Nova.

16

'Okay, pal,' the gunman told Lin, goading him with the tip of his weapon. 'Up on your feet. Let's go, you're coming with us.'

Lin rose to his knees, shivering with fear. Looking away from the gun, he finally recognized the man who had called out to him in the restaurant.

'BA!'

'Shut up and get in the car!' The gunman grabbed Lin by the shirt and jerked him over to the limousine. The rear door was still open, and Lin reluctantly climbed into the plush confines of the back seat. The gunman followed, then paused to send more bullets zinging just above the heads of the A-Team. 'If you know what's good for you, you'll stay put till we're long gone from here.'

'Should we close our eyes and count to a hundred?' Hannibal whispered bitterly under his breath as he heard the limo door slam shut.

'I ain't scared of that fool's popgun,' BA growled as the limousine backed out of the parking lot, almost crashing into a vintage Stutz Bearcat. While the driver of the Bearcat was throwing a tantrum and leaning on his horn, BA jumped to his feet and used the cover of parked vehicles to reach the front sidewalk. The man with the Uzi spotted him and sprayed a round of ammo as the limo's driver pulled out into traffic. The burst of gunfire stitched several cars, but BA reached his van unscathed, and by the time Lin's abductors had run their first red light a half-block away, Baracus was behind the wheel and gunning his engine into life. The rest of the A-Team rushed to join him.

'All right,' Hannibal said, taking the front seat. 'Let's play catch-up!'

'Damn right!' BA eased up on the clutch and the van lurched from its parking space, weaving through the congested intersection and managing to stay within sight of the racing limousine.

'I wonder who those guys were?' Face said, brushing the dirt from his suit. 'And how'd they show up the same time we did?'

'Karma,' Murdock speculated. 'I'm sure if I'd had time to

consult the Ching before you guys picked me up this morning, I would have come up with a reading –'

'Shut it or I'll shut it for you, sucker!' BA shouted over his shoulder. 'I ain't in the mood for your crazy talk now!'

'Whoever they were, they were obviously after Lin,' Hannibal said, 'and I don't think they were just after a look at his green card.'

'Are you guys positive it was him?' Amy asked, still catching her breath. 'I mean, it was ten years ago, after –'

'Of course it was him!' BA cut in. 'You saw how he jumped when I shouted his name back in the restaurant.'

'I'd rather you didn't remind me about that, BA,' Face groaned. 'I'll never be able to use that place again, thanks to that charming display you put on for the folks there.'

'Well, you'll have to use that mystery penthouse you've been holing up in the past few weeks, eh, Face?' Hannibal cracked, starting to work on one of his patented cigars. 'How we doin', BA?'

'I still see 'em,' BA wrestled with the steering wheel as he kept up the van's speed, cutting corners to keep from falling too far behind the limousine. The chase carried over to side streets that ran through the residential district tucked a few blocks in from the tarnished glitter of Sunset Boulevard and Hollywood proper. Small, quaint houses with manicured lawns and adobe tile roofs lined the quiet streets. A few sprinklers were running, but that was the only sign of activity except for the few other cars making the rounds through the neighbourhood.

'"Ay-yi-yi",' Murdock said. 'Did you hear him say "Ay-yi-yi"? He said "Ay-yi-yi".'

'Yeah,' BA recalled. 'Only Lin says "Ay-yi-yi" like that.'

'What?' Amy said. 'What are you talking about?'

'Murdock taught Lin to sing Western songs while we were being held in the prison camp,' Hannibal told her. 'You know, "Home on the Range" kinda stuff. The chorus to "The Chisolm Trail" goes: "Come-a-ti-yi-yipee-yipee-ay-yipee-ay". Lin loved that song, but he could never get it right. He always ended up singing "Ay-yi-yi".'

'That's because Murdock didn't teach it to him right,' BA

18

insisted. 'That's how we know it's him for sure.'

'I did so teach him right,' Murdock claimed.

'Did not,' BA maintained.

'Did too.'

BA reached behind him and grabbed Murdock by the collar. 'Say what?'

'You're right,' Murdock confessed sheepishly. 'Did not.'

'Hey, what is this, "the Shari Lewis show", guys?' Hannibal intervened. 'Cut it out, both of you. BA, keep your eyes on the road and make sure those goons don't get away from us.'

BA rounded a corner, then quickly pumped on the van's brakes. 'Man, where did they go?'

They had come to a point where the road forked out in three directions. The limousine couldn't be seen down any of the offshoot streets.

'Great!' Face said dismally. 'What now?'

Murdock wondered aloud, 'Anybody remember how to play "Eenie Meenie"...?'

THREE

'I do nothing!' Lin Duk Coo protested as he watched the scenery whiz by in a blur through the limo windows. 'Let me go! I am Peter Pereime, only a poor chef with a –'

'Shut up!' the man beside him ordered, ramming the tip of his Uzi into Lin's ribs. 'We know damn well who you are, so don't lay that poor chef song-and-dance bit on us.'

Lin eased away from the gun barrel, eyeing his captor hatefully. 'Who are you?'

'I told you to shut up! You want a gag, keep it running and you'll have a mouth full of necktie, got it?' With his free hand, the gunman reached for his collar and began loosening the knot of his tie. Lin took the cue and fell silent, trying to figure out how these men had managed to track him down. He really hadn't needed to ask who the men were. He knew only too well.

The driver peered into the rear-view mirror, inspecting the trickle of traffic behind them for a trace of the A-Team's black van. Not seeing it, he grinned and shifted his gaze to take in the prisoner in the back seat. 'The boss will be plenty pleased to see you, shortstuff. I'm sure he's gonna want to repay you for all the times you slipped through his fingers.'

Lin said nothing. He stared down glumly at his knees, cursing himself silently for having run from the restaurant before looking to see who'd been calling to him. If he'd taken the mere second he would have needed to recognize BA, he would have been in the company of the A-Team when these henchmen showed up. If anyone could have kept him from falling into the hands of his sworn enemies, it was Hannibal Smith, Templeton Peck, BA Baracus, and Howling Mad

20

Murdock. As it was, they still had almost managed to rescue him before the limo driver had lost them on the side streets. If if if. Almost almost almost. None of that mattered now. After a brief taste of unburdened freedom, Lin Duk Coo felt sure that his past had finally caught up with him, and that it was now only a matter of time before he would lose his liberty, if not his life.

They were out of the residential district now, and entering an industrial park area. Factories and warehouses stood idle on the Sunday afternoon, their only sound being that of generators keeping the interior bowls functioning until the frenetic pace of the workweek would resume the following morning. The limousine slowed down as it rolled through the heart of the complex, then pulled off the main road and paused before a locked gate leading to a parking lot filled with powder-blue delivery trucks that were aligned in neat rows next to buildings of the same colour. Lettering on the sides of both the trucks and the buildings proclaimed this to be the domain of the Angel Bread Company. Lin's guard handed his submachine gun to the driver, then got out and unlocked the gates. He swung them open long enough for the limousine to pull into the parking lot and disappear around the corner of the first warehouse. Once he'd closed the gate and locked it, the man in the blue suit checked the streets a final time, then headed off in the direction the limo had taken behind the warehouse.

Less than a minute later, a semi-truck rumbled past the bakery, flanked on the right by the A-Team's black van. Behind the wheel, BA was keeping a steady foot on the accelerator, matching the semi's speed in such a way that anyone who might have been watching the road from the bakery would have only seen the larger truck. Once they were a few dozen yards down the road, BA pulled off onto the shoulder and eased the van into a cramped place of concealment behind an ungroomed cluster of budding camellias.

'Lucky guess, Murdock,' Hannibal said as BA turned off the engine. 'If we'd taken the wrong way, there's no way we would have spotted them before they pulled off the road.'

21

Murdock held up his pinkie and ring finger. 'I couldn't have done it without Eenie and Meenie.'

Face peered out the back doors of the van at the building where their friend had been taken. 'Angel Bread Company? I know Lin makes a great loaf, but I can't believe someone would go to this much trouble just to get a recipe out of him.'

'I think there's only one way we're going to find out,' Hannibal said, climbing out of the van and circling around to the back. Opening the rear doors, he started handing out a variety of weapons to the other members of the team. 'Okay, we don't know what's going on here, so we're going to have to stay loose.'

'Don't we always?' Face said, taking a M-16 and slapping the stock for good luck.

'Loose like a goose, sauce or no sauce,' Murdock rambled as Hannibal gave him a high-powered rifle.

'Quit talkin' about food, man!' BA complained. 'We still ain't eaten, 'cept for a few bites of bread!'

'Now, who's fault is that, BA?' Face said. 'If you hadn't opened your yap and started this whole ruckus, we could be downing chocolate mousse after a five-course feast.'

'If we're lucky, maybe they're passing out free breadsticks at the bakery,' Hannibal said. Giving Amy an automatic pistol, he told her, 'You're on the wheel, kid. After we come out, pull this in as close as you can and be ready to roll.'

Amy nodded and held her hand out for BA to give her the keys. BA was wary of letting them go, though. 'Careful with my van. I just got it fixed up after what Hannibal did to it down in San Pedro. He about totalled it driving it off that pier!'

'Better the van than us,' Hannibal reminded him.

'Don't worry, BA,' Amy assured him, 'I'll drive it like it was my own, I promise.'

As Amy climbed back into the van and made her way to the driver's seat, the men huddled briefly behind the vehicle, eyeing their objective across the street.

'Face, you get the right flank. I'll take the centre,' Hannibal said. 'BA, you flank left. Murdock, you're the rear guard on a hundred count. When we retreat, you crank up a

22

cross-fire if we need it.'

'Gotcha, Colonel,' Murdock said brightly, snapping off a crisp salute.

'Oh, man,' BA grimaced, 'Don't let no crazy man be on cross-fire, Hannibal. This fool'll gun us all down by mistake thinkin' he's Sergeant York or some damn thing!'

'It's just a cover position in case we get in trouble, BA,' Hannibal said. 'And we're not gonna get in trouble.'

BA scoffed, grasping his rifle tightly.

'Think of it this way, BA,' Face joked as they started across the street. 'If Murdock stays behind, he won't be able to get your goose any more, right?'

BA glared at Face. 'Man, I got nutbars all around me. C'mon, let's get this over with...'

As Hannibal advanced towards the main gate, Face and BA broke off and headed for spots on opposite sides of the bakery. A large cyclone fence surrounded the property, and taut lengths of barbed-wire extended a few feet higher as an additional deterrent against intrusion. Reaching the gate, Hannibal blew a plume of smoke from his cigar as he slipped out of his suit jacket and unbuttoned the matching waistcoat to give him more mobility. Slinging his rifle over his shoulder, he tossed the coat up so that it landed over a section of the barbed-wire barrier.

'Perfect,' he murmured to himself. 'Keep that up and you'll be ready for the rodeo circuit.'

Hannibal checked to see Peck and BA sizing up the fence far down to his right and left, then took a few steps back and drew in a deep breath. Charging forward, he flung himself at the fence, then used his momentum to climb within reach of the coat. After taking another breath, he pulled himself over the barbed-wire and dropped with a cat-like pounce to the asphalt of the parking lot. Unslinging his rifle, he crouched over and ran to the cover of the nearest delivery truck.

'So far so good,' he whispered. 'Now's when it gets tricky.'

With the precision stealth of trained commandos, Hannibal, Peck, and BA darted from truck to truck, moving closer to the building and closer to one another. Hannibal was the first one around the corner of the main warehouse, and he quickly sprang behind a trash bin to avoid being spotted by two armed men who were standing near the loading dock of the bakery, transferring racks of freshly-made bread into the back of a delivery truck parked next to the vacated limousine.

A hundred feet away, Peck rounded the other back corner of the building and likewise was forced to make a fast dash for cover upon spotting the gunmen. Peering around the stacked crates he was hiding behind, Face made eye contact with Hannibal and pointed to his right. Hannibal looked where Peck was pointing and saw an archway on the other side of the trash bin. Once he was sure that the gunmen were preoccupied with loading bread into the truck, Hannibal slipped away from the bin and passed through the archway to an inner hallway. A lone door was centred at the end of the hall, and as Hannibal headed for it, he suddenly sensed someone moving up on him from behind. Slipping his index finger over the metallic curve of his rifle's trigger, Hannibal lunged to one side and spun around. Only well-honed instincts kept him from reflexively gunning down BA, who froze in place, staring fitfully down the bore of the weapon aimed at his face.

'Sorry, BA,' Hanibal whispered, lowering his rifle.

'Pretty fast move, Hannibal,' BA replied, managing a grin. 'You haven't lost your stuff.'

As the two of them approached the door, Hannibal murmured, 'I got a feeling it's locked. You bring along your little helpers?'

BA nodded, retrieving a locksmith's kit from his vest pocket. As he moved over and went to work on the lock, Hannibal kept watch over the hallway for signs of activity. They were able to break into the building without incident. Inside, there were more corridors, all of them dimly lit because the bakery was supposedly closed for the day. A lingering aroma of fresh dough hung in the air, however.

'What now?' BA wondered quietly.

Hannibal didn't answer. He cocked his head to one side and put a finger to his lips. BA listened intently, then he could hear it too – voices, coming from the large receiving room adjacent to the loading docks. Side by side, the two men padded down the hall and came to a stop next to the opened doorway leading to the chamber where their friend was being harassed by the gunman who had apprehended him outside the restaurant.

'I guess you know you're dead, shorty.'

Lin Duk Coo was seated on a crate, his hands now tied behind his back. He levelled his gaze at the man in the dark suit and spat. 'A threat from one without authority is not to be feared. You talk like a big man, but you take orders from someone else.'

'Oh yeah? The man in the suit lashed out with the back of his hand, slapping Lin across the face. 'You see me asking anyone if it was all right to do that? Huh?'

Lin's head snapped to one side as he rolled with the blow, which left red welts on his cheek. He refused to acknowledge any pain, though. Clenching his teeth, he remained silent and looked at the floor, ready to endure whatever future indignities might be in store for him.

There were two other entrances to the receiving room besides the one Hannibal and BA were stationed next to. The driver of the limousine came in through the door closest to the loading docks and called out to his partner, 'Mr Anderson says we should take him out with the load and feed him to the crabs.'

Lin's tormentor beamed at this news. Grabbing the chef by the chin, he tilted Lin's face up so that their eyes locked, then taunted, 'In case you don't *comprende*, that's the authority to waste your butt! What do you think of that?'

'I think that it is a shame I must die by the hands of mindless fools,' Lin declared. 'Go ahead, hit me again while my hands are tied behind my back! Coward!'

The gunman held himself back from striking Lin again, although his face was flushed with rage. Going over to a nearby work bench, he grabbed a roll of packing tape, fuming, 'I'm not gonna waste my tie gagging you, egg roll. I'll tape your yap shut once and for all, and if you give me any more trouble, I'll plug your nose, too, and you can die nice and slow from suffocation.'

25

'Just bring the tape and do it once we're on the way,' the driver said. 'The truck's about loaded already and Anderson wants us out of here, pronto.'

The gunman ripped off a length of tape. 'At least let me put this much on him.'

Before the adhesive could be applied to Lin's mouth, a rattle of gunfire echoed through the room and the area around the chef and his abductors began to look like a shooting gallery in full swing. Bullets ripped into the walls and skimmed across the floor, prompting the kidnappers to perform what looked to be some sort of interpretive stork dance.

Hannibal and BA followed their barrage into the receiving room, then let their guns go silent.

'Okay boys,' Hannibal advised the culprits, 'Down with your guns and up with your hands or we're the ones who'll be wasting butts.'

'You guys!' the limo driver cried, recognizing Hannibal and BA. 'Couldn't stay away, could you?'

Hannibal shook his head, still biting on his cigar. 'You ran off with the chef before we could give him our compliments. Bad etiquette. We'll have to teach you some manners.'

'Hannibal!' Lin howled with relief. 'BA!'

'Howdy, Lin,' Hannibal said. 'Long time, no bread, eh?'

Hannibal's cocky banter came at the expense of needed caution, and neither he or BA saw another gunman appear in the third doorway. Fortunately, the man fired with too much haste to be accurate, and Hannibal was able to lurch clear of the shots, at the same time knocking BA out of harm's way. Lin took advantage of the disruption to jump up from the crate and ram his shoulder into the midsection of the man in the dark suit. Staggering into his partner, the man shouted harmless profanities at Lin, who scampered away to join Hannibal and BA as they were retreating into a maze of bread racks to avoid the next fusillade and make their way toward the loading docks.

Outside the building, the two men loading the last rack of bread into the delivery truck heard the explosions coming from the receiving room and quickly grabbed their guns to lend a hand. Before they could get inside, though, Peck let loose with his rifle and pinned the men against an alcove a few yards from the archway through which Hannibal and BA had entered the bakery. Breaking away from the crates, Peck ran across the parking lot, covering his advance with the last of his ammunition. When he reached the delivery truck, he bounded in behind the steering wheel and started up the engine. Just as he was getting ready to pull away, Hannibal and BA burst out of the building with Lin Duk Coo close behind.

Sticking his head out the window, Peck shouted, 'Get in, you guys! We're outta here!'

Hannibal fired a round at the two gunmen in the alcove, giving BA and Lin enough time to clamber into the back of the delivery truck. As Peck drove off, Hannibal caught up with him on the run and pulled himself up into the passenger's side of the vehicle just as a stream of bullets hammered into the ground where he'd been standing seconds before.

'Nice job, Face,' Hannibal said between breaths. 'As the hippies say, keep on truckin'!'

The engine was incredibly sluggish compared to the responsiveness of the van, but by constantly keeping the accelerator floored and steering sharply to avoid collision with the other trucks, Face was able to build up enough speed to elude the men who were pursuing them on foot from behind. At some point, a guard wandered out to the main gate to investigate the suit coat hanging over the barbed-wire, and when he heard the delivery truck approaching, he whipped out his pistol and stood his ground before the gate. Raising his gun, he shouted, 'Stop or I shoot!'

It didn't take more than a few seconds for the guard to realize that Peck had no intention of stopping. As the truck was almost upon him, he dived to one side, inadvertently bringing a stack of skids crashing down on himself. The force of the truck's speeding bulk wrenched the gate from its hinges, sending it flying off to one side as Face gripped the steering wheel hard to keep the vehicle under control.

Murdock was perched atop the A-Team's van, armed with

27

the high-powered rifle. As Amy realized that it was Peck in the delivery truck and quickly eased the van to one side to allow the others to race by, Murdock drew a bead on the limousine, which had just appeared around the corner of the warehouse and was speeding towards the gateway. There was a full cartridge of ammo in the rifle, and by the time he'd emptied it, Murdock had effectively destroyed both the limo's front tyres, as well as its radiator and engine block. Spewing steam, the luxury vehicle slumped to the asphalt like a downed bull that had been felled in the arena. Its occupants scrambled out and took a series of potshots at Lin Duk Coo's liberators, but by then both the van and the delivery truck were far off down the road.

'Heeeeeeeeahhhhhh!' Murdock howled, clinging to the rooftop of the van. 'Ride 'em, cowboy!'

'Oh, oh,' Hannibal mumbled, staring out the window of the delivery truck at Murdock's effusive performance atop the van. 'I think we've got the Range Rider back for a quick encore!'

'If it wasn't my van, I'd tell Amy to shake him, loose,' BA sneered.

'Now, now, BA,' Hannibal said. 'Give Murdock a little credit. After all, he didn't nail you in his cross-fire, did he?'

'Damn fool didn't have a chance to!' BA countered.

Hannibal relaxed in the back of the truck, taking out a fresh cigar to replace the one he'd lost during their getaway. 'What d'ya say, Lin?' he cracked, 'I'll bet ... Lin?'

Lin Duk Coo was slumped into a sitting position next to the loaded bread racks, but his eyes were closed and his head tilted oddly to one side. BA noticed that something was wrong at the same time and both men scrambled to the chef's side.

'Hey, Hannibal, he's out cold!'

Hannibal looked Lin over. 'He hasn't been shot from what I can see.'

'What's wrong?' Face cried out from the driver's seat.

'Never mind, just keep driving!' Hannibal shouted back. Lin's out cold, but we don't know what happened to –'

'Here, check out his head, man,' BA said, running a hand

over the chef's close-cropped hair. 'He's got a lump here like an Easter egg. Musta banged his brain into that bread rack when he was hopping into the truck.'

Hannibal inspected the bruise. 'That's a beaut all right. He's going to be in dreamland for awhile.'

'Damn!' BA muttered. 'I was hopin' we'd get some answers about what's going on with him.'

'Well, it's gonna have to wait,' Hannibal said, easing Lin into a more comfortable position before moving up next to Face in the front of the truck. 'In the meantime, I think we need to lay low so our fan club at the bakery doesn't find us. Face, is there an underground garage at this joint where you're staying?'

'Oh no, uh uh,' Face said, shaking his head furiously. 'Look, I've got a good gig goin' there, and I'm not going to blow it by bringing you guys around. Nothing personal, but one botched connection in one day is enough for me.'

'Tell me something, Face,' Hannibal said through a mouthful of smoke. 'What's your rank, last time you checked.'

'He's a lieutenant,' BA prompted from the back. 'And you're a Colonel, Hannibal. You're the boss!'

'Thanks, BA,' Hannibal smirked. 'Now, then, Face, what was that you were saying about showing us your place...?'

FOUR

They used to say that geographic necessity made cities like New York and Chicago grow vertically with an unending profusion of skyscrapers, while the vast expanse of developable land surrounding Los Angeles allowed that metropolis to grow outwards in every direction except into the ocean. To a large extent, the saying has held true, as each decade has found the suburbs of LA edging further and further from the heart of the city, like the probing false feet of a bulging amoeba. And yet, there are those stretches throughout that coastal centre where high-rise buildings have sprouted like toadstools in the wake of heavy rain. Particularly prolific has been the Wilshire Corridor, running westward from downtown all the way to Santa Monica and the sands of the Pacific. Although a fair share of the skyscrapers spaced along this boulevard lease their space to businesses, the overwhelming majority fall into the category of luxury condominiums. For anywhere from a couple of hundred thousand dollars on up to a few million, the wealthier of LA's residents can opt for the convenience of the upright neighbourhood, where there are no lawn chores to contend with and a supposedly ever-vigilant security force on duty to see that Jehovah's Witnesses, insurance peddlers, and other door-to-door salesmen don't intrude upon one's private space.

Templeton Peck resided in one such condominium, a twelve-storey structure of concrete and mirrored glass, surrounded by grounds that were kept up by hired gardeners, and a spike-topped wrought iron fence that was in the process of being hidden from view by fast-growing bougainvillaea and creeping fig. They called the place Century Towers West, and, appropriately, there was a similar-looking building next door called Century Towers East, making the two complexes look like high-tech rooks in a chess set for Paul Bunyan.

Lin Duk Coo was just coming to when Face drove the delivery truck into the subterranean garage located beneath the twin towers. Amy followed close behind in the black van, with Murdock now safely inside the vehicle. They parked in a pair of adjacent spots within view of the elevators. Lin stirred and blinked his eyes open. He was disoriented, and it was several seconds before he recognized the men with him. By that time Amy and Murdock had come over and opened the back doors of the delivery truck to let them out.

'Oh boy! I get rescued in the nick of time,' Lin blubbered excitedly as BA helped him out. 'Thank you!'

'If you'd looked before you ran you'd have seen us, man,' BA told him.

'Yes, yes.' Lin nodded his head vigorously, then winced as the motion aggravated the throbbing pain in his skull. He forced a smile at BA as he dabbed a finger against the knot on his head. 'You are one hard man to miss.'

'It looks like the years have treated you well,' Face said, stepping forward to give the chef a warm hug. 'It's good to see you, Lin.'

'I say the same to you . . . all of you. You saved my life back at the bakery.' Lin traded more embraces with the other members of the A-Team and shook Amy's hand earnestly when he was introduced to her.

'What's goin on, Lin?' Hannibal asked once the greetings were all taken care of.

'I'm in big trouble,' Lin said, his smile fading. 'Old ghosts have come to haunt me.'

'Pretty real ghosts from the looks of it,' Hannibal said.

Before Lin could go into more detail, a Rolls Royce, one of several in the garage, pulled into the parking spot next to the van. A married couple in their mid-fifties, both dressed in tailored clothes made to complement their greying heads, got out of the vehicle and looked with concern at the group before them.

'Mr Toney?' the husband asked Face. 'Everything all right?'

While the others looked around for the mysterious Mr Toney, Face offered the couple a bright smile. 'Just fine, Dr Peters.' Seeing that Mrs Peters was still unsettled by the presence of his associates, Peck adlibbed, 'These people are helping to install Mrs Wright's sixteenth floor L unit. Wait until you see it. It's a little piece of heaven.'

'Outstanding,' Dr Peters boomed with relief.

'Oh, Mr Toney,' Mrs Peters called out before her husband could whisk her away to the elevators. 'We do hope you're still planning on that brunch we told you about last week.'

'Oh, absolutely, Mrs Peters. I wouldn't miss it for the world.' Peck grinned slyly at the woman. 'You know me better than that, now don't you?'

'Careful, Mr Toney,' the doctor chuckled. 'You're making my wife blush.'

'Forgive me.'

As the couple walked off, arm in arm, lasping back into the conversation they'd been nursing before encountering the A-Team, Hannibal looked over at Peck. 'Mr Toney? You gotta be kidding!'

'Sounds like some hairdresser,' BA mocked.

'Mr Toney...' Amy muttered, trying to place the name. 'Isn't he the famous LA decorator?'

'Look, can we get out of the garage, please?' Peck pleaded. 'If I give you guys half a chance you'll blow my cover and we'll all be living the low life.'

BA looked around at the Jaguars, Bentleys, and Mercedes that accompanied the Rolls Royces in the parking structure. 'Buncha high rollers hangin' out here. How'd you wrangle your way in here, Face?'

Seeing that the Peters had just disappeared behind the sliding doors of one of the elevators, Face said, 'Let's just go to my penthouse suite, all right? And try to show a little class, would ya? We're talkin' upper crust here.'

'Lead on, your Lieutenantness,' Hannibal said drolly, plucking a fresh cigar from his pocket. 'Don't worry, I won't light it in the elevator.'

Face led the others to the elevator and pushed the 'up' button, then asked Lin, 'Okay, we're all dying to know... how'd you manage to make it from Nam to here?'

Lin grinned and tapped his forehead. 'Count on a good cook to also be a sharp cookie. I get out of country... how you say, by hook or crook?'

'Hook or crook,' Hannibal corrected. 'At least, I doubt you used a hooker to get out.'

A bell rang out and the doors to the left elevator hissed open, revealing yet another wealthy couple, these two a few years younger than Mr and Mrs Peters but no less well-dressed.

'Hi, Mrs Kline, Mr Kline,' Face blurted out, injecting charm into his voice. When the Klines warily stepped out of the elevator and looked over the A-Team, particularly BA, Face addressed his cohorts with sudden harshness. 'How many times have I told you, when you deliver a crushed velvet sofa you must wear white gloves. You left fingerprints where you carried it.'

As the Klines headed off for their BMW, the others slipped into the elevator. Once the doors had closed and Peck had pushed for the top floor, Lin gave off a short laugh and said. 'Faceman does not change. Still scam like crazy.'

'We all have our calling,' Peck said as they started up.

'A decorator?' BA snorted. 'You jivin' these folks that you're a decorator?'

'I love it,' Amy snickered. 'Tony Curtis could take lessons from you, Face. Tell me, is this front you're putting on going to give you some sense of taste?'

'I can't believe what I'm hearing!' Peck complained. 'I'm risking the cushiest gig I've latched onto in years to hide you guys out and what do I get for thanks? Insults! It's enough to make a guy think about going solo.'

'Aw, c'mon, Face, take a joke, will ya?' Hannibal said, setting a match to his cigar.

'You said you weren't going to light that thing in the elevator,' Face reminded him.

'You're right. My mistake.' Hannibal handed the match to

BA, who held it long enough for Hannibal to get the cigar going.

Face looked at Lin and shook his head. 'Tough break, Lin. You bargained on help and you got comedians...'

FIVE

It wasn't the Presidential suite, but the five penthouse rooms Templeton Peck called home would have suited most royalty with their lavish accommodations. From plush carpeting as thick as a Rockefeller's wallet to walls filled with prints and paintings that rivalled the collections in some of the city's more prestigious art galleries, the apartment was a marvel of extravagance, begging for a photographic tour by the staff shutterbugs of Architectural Digest. There was a placard on an easel in the front hallway giving credit to the true perpetrator of this lap of luxury, and as he let the others gape at the surroundings, Peck discreetly removed the sign and hid it behind an overstuffed sofa in the living room.

'Face, this is incredible!' Amy gawked, taking a close look at one of two Ming vases perched on either side of a bronze gong resting atop the fireplace mantle. 'You've really outdone yourself this time.'

'How'd you scam this place anyway, sucker?' BA muttered. 'I'm livin' at some sleazy motel and you're in a damn palace!'

'Look, can we put the apartment behind us?' Face moved over and grabbed the blown-glass figurine of a ballerina that BA had picked up from the end table. 'Why don't we just get down to business? I think we need to find out why those guys are trying to kill Lin.'

No one seemed interested in Peck's proposal. Amy began browsing the walls, admiring the artwork, while Lin wandered into the kitchen and covertously eyed the plethora of cooking utensils. Murdock sat down on the sofa next to BA and picked up a bonsai tree from the table. After sniffing the fragrance of the miniature leaves, Murdock began grazing on them, pinching off small clusters as if they were some sort of imported bon bons.

Hannibal had seen Peck hide the sign when they'd entered the apartment, and he nonchalantly retrieved it, holding it out at arm's length to read:

MODEL PENTHOUSE APARTMENT
DESIGNED BY MR A. TONEY,
CUSTOM INTERIOR DECORATOR

'I love this, Face,' Hannibal said, setting the sign aside and moving away from the sofa to take in the view through a large sliding glass door that led to an outside terrace. 'You're okay, kid. This is my kinda action.'

'I'm glad you approve,' Face replied sarcastically. 'My mother always told me that anything worth doing was worth doing well.'

'I thought you were an orphan since you were a baby,' Murdock said between munches of bonsai.

Hannibal blew a cloud of smoke and continued his exploration of the living room as he continued to give Peck a hard time. 'Here you are, livin in Mr Toney's plush-pile playpen, bumming brunches with Dr and Mrs Peters... sleeping in Mr Toney's silk jammies.' Hannibal hoisted the pyjamas from the chair they were draped over and waved them like a victory flag. 'Yessir, I'm proud of you, Face. And, as the leader of the A-Team, I'm gonna commandeer this joint as my temporary command headquarters.'

As Hannibal sealed his decision with a peal of the mantle gong, Peck threw his hands up with resignation. 'Great. Just great. Try and help out and you get used and abused. Okay, gang, go ahead and make yourselves at home. Just remember, though... you break anything, you bought it.'

'All I want is some food, man,' BA said, grabbing an apple from a basket of fruit on the coffee table. He bit into it and promptly made a face, realizing the apple was made of wax.

'Gee, BA, I'm real sorry about that,' Peck drawled. 'I guess it isn't ripe yet, huh.'

BA spat the wax out and rose to his feet, shouting to Lin in the kitchen, 'Hey, is there some real food in there?'

Lin had alrady checked the cupboards. As he opened the refrigerator door, Face said, 'There's not much in there, either, Lin. Look, BA, this place is a demo. Get it? It's for show. I'm not about to load up on groceries and risk blowing my cover. Hell, most of the time I have to wait until after midnight to slip in so folks don't know I'm sleeping here.'

'We all have our crosses to bear,' Hannibal said. 'Look, I saw a deli just down the street on our way here. Amy, do you think you could go grab some take-out while we have a little reunion pow-wow with Lin?'

'Sure.'

Amy took orders and left the penthouse. Because the A-Team was wary of Lin's abductors possibly being on the prowl in the neighbourhood, Amy didn't want to risk being spotted in the van, so she had to go to the deli on foot. It was more than forty-five minutes before she returned, and by then Lin Duk Coo was well into his narrative about the events in his life since the time he'd last seen Hannibal and the others.

'... I come to America,' he was saying. 'Genral Kao, he arrange it for me. He say to me, contact Mr Anderson at Angel Bread Company, give him a letter, which is what I do.'

Amy set the bag of food on the coffee table, and there was a mometary lull in the conversation as everyone grabbed for their orders and began eating.

'I hope you guys don't think I'm going to write this off as a business expense at the newspaper,' Amy said, holding an opened palm out. 'Pay up, everybody but Lin. Lin, treat's on me.'

'Thank you, Miss Allen. Much obliged.' Lin took a few bites from the submarine sandwich he's ordered, waiting for the others to finish passing money to Amy for their meals, then continued with his story. 'Mr Anderson, he turn out to be Lieutenant Angel from POW camp.'

'That creep from 'C' barracks?' Murdock sputtered, talking through the mouthful of pastrami he'd got to go with his bonsai. 'That slime Navy lieutenant who burned everybody? Mr Snitch?'

'And isn't General Kao that sadist you were telling me

about at the restaurant?' Amy mentioned. 'Why would he help Lin escape from his own prison camp?'

'You'd have to know Kao personally and you'd know he'd have had his reasons,' Hannibal said. 'He always had the clout and moxie to do what he wanted. Obviously he wanted Lin to deliver a message to this Lieutenant Angel, who was not only the biggest scumbag in the whole camp while we were there, but a collaborator with the enemy too. Kao and Angel were two peas in a pod.'

'And now Angel goes by the name of Anderson?' Amy said.

'Right, and apparently he either owns or runs the bakery we just yanked Lin from.' Hannibal turned to the chef. 'What else do you know? Did you know what was in the letter?'

Lin shook his head. 'Letter was sealed. I give it up before I know Mr Anderson is Lieutenant Angel. At first I think it is letter of recommendation to give me a job, because before I find out about Angel, the man I give letter to come back from boss's office and offers me job at bakery. I work less than one day when I hear word that they want to kill me and make it look like accident. I take off just in time and wander around city, not knowing what to do. Finally I find some fellow countrymen who put me up, get me job at Arkan's. I guess today they find out about me, try to kill me for good.'

'They won't hurt you as long as we have anything to say about it, Lin,' Hannibal told him. 'I think it'd be best if you stayed with us for the time being, too. No telling whether or not they've got the place where you're staying staked out.'

'It's good to have good friends,' Lin observed. 'I don't know how to thank you.'

'I do,' Face said, setting down his ham-on-rye. 'Once things cool down, maybe you can cook up one of your specialities. That bread at the restaurant brought back memories.'

'You got a deal,' Lin promised. 'What you had at camp was nothing. Wait till you taste what I can make when I have choice of ingredients!'

'Man, now you're talkin',' BA said.

As the others finished eating, Hannibal chewed slowly on his roast beef sub, staring contemplatively out the window. He finally murmured, 'If General Kao and Angel are in cahoots after all these years, something important's got to be going down. I wonder what it is...?'

SIX

Tom Angel had made a token effort to live a clean life back in the sixties, managing to make it half-way through college without running foul of the law. However, as he was struggling through his junior year, Tom found the lure of extra-curricular activities too tempting to resist. He'd periodically bought small quantities of marijuana and broken them down into ounce packets to sell to friends and acquaintances for enough of a profit to forestall the need to pursue an honest living, but that year he'd got chummy with a big supplier and had stepped-up his dealing to the point where instead of worrying about graduating from college, he was more concerned about graduating from pounds to kilos. In effort to expand his clientele, he became a little less cautious about advertising his sideline enterprise. It was a typical mistake made by hundreds like him at the time, and it had the typical repercussion. There came the day when he made a sale to undercover narcotics agents and found himself hauled from his dormitory to the local city jail on charges of peddling pot. As Tom's luck would have it, his father was an organized crime figure who was in no way interested in getting tangled up in his son's problems. It would have been easy enough for Roger Angel to pull a few strings and have his son released without so much as a blemish on his record, but the old man refused to so much as post Tom's bail, and as a result the young man was faced wth one of the famous 'either-or' propositions of the time. Either he could enlist in the Armed Forces and go to Vietnam or he could be sent to the state pen for a minimum of five to ten years. Thus Thomas Angel began the tour of duty that would see him finagle his way through the ranks until he came home in 1974 as a lieutenant with an honourable discharge and a Purple Heart he'd bought for a bundle of Thai sticks the size of a small log. He'd learned enough about the ways of corruption overseas to impress his father, and for the past eight years he'd been acting as Roger Angel's LA connection, using the bread company as a front for the various illegal activities he'd developed a prowess for.

Tom enjoyed his position and the comforts it afforded him. He had bodyguards and a limousine at his disposal, and he could indulge himself in fine clothes, fast women, and any vice that struck his fancy at any given moment.

But it wasn't enough. Tom had grown tired of handling affairs limited to the Los Angeles area. He wanted to expand his territory. He wanted the whole state to play with. And the day Lin Duk Coo had arrived at the bakery with a hand-written proposition from his old war buddy, General Kao, Angel had seen his opportunity. Over the past few weeks he had put together all the needed connections and arrangements for the big operation he thought would inevitably project him into the next higher realm of authority in the family business.

And then had come the Sunday string of circumstances that threatened to undo not only his many preparations, but also the very fabric of his localized empire. He had literally put all his money on the venture with General Kao, and unless something was done to remedy the damage that had been done in the wake of Lin Duk Coo's escape from the bakery, Angel would be wiped out financially, if not physically as well. He was caught up in a high-stake game, and the odds had taken an alarming shift against his favour.

'When are we going to be there?' he shouted impatiently from the back seat of his limousine.

The two men who had abducted Lin Duk Coo from the restaurant the day before were in the front seat. The gunman in the blue suit glanced back at his boss and told him, 'In a few minutes. We're almost at the exit now.'

They were travelling on the northbound freeway, heading away from the city and suburbs and towards the relative

41

barrenness of Antelope Valley. It was shortly after dawn, and the cloudless sky was brightening by the second, in direct proportion to the increasing darkness of Angel's mood. He opened the door of the mini-cooler built into the back seat and pulled out a small container of orange juice. There were only a few swallows left, and before putting them down, Angel took a silver flask from his suit jacket and poured in a few ounces of vodka. The drink surged through his system, simultaneously hot and cold, giving him a jolt that served to bolster his confidence. He knew that he would have to assume the offensive in the upcoming confrontation with General Kao. This was not a time to show weakness.

Angel took a final sip from the flask before putting it back in his jacket and lighting up a cigarette to mask the smell of liquor on his breath. He was already feeling looser, and by the time the limousine had left the freeway and taken the side road leading to a secluded wash, he felt in command.

'Here we are, chief,' the driver said, pulling to a stop near the concrete framework of the wash. 'Right on schedule.'

'Glad to see it,' Angel replied, stubbing out his cigarette. He waited for the other man to get out and open his door, then he emerged from the limo, tightening his tie and taking in a deep breath of the smog-free air. He looked around, seeing a few scattered oaks and clumps of manzanita dotting the terrain around the wash. A range of mountains rose in the distance, providing the backdrop behind which the sun made its first appearance of the day.

Just as Angel was about to inspect his watch, he heard the faint droning of rotors. Screening the sun's glare with the back of his hand, he looked in the direction of the sound and saw a small speck in the sky grow into the outline of a small helicopter. The whirr of the chopper grew louder as it approached the wash and hovered in the air a few seconds before descending to a clearing two dozen yards from the limousine. Angel took a few steps away from the car, just far enough to be beyond earshot of his henchmen, then stood his ground.

'Let him come to me,' he whispered to himself.

The helicopter pilot left the engine running as the

passenger's door opened and a short man in a white silk suit disembarked. Crouching over to stay clear of the spinning blades, General Kao made his way to Tom Angel. Bald and tanned, Kao looked more like an oriental entrepreneur than a military figure who had amassed an incredible fortune over the years by using his prestigious position to establish a crime network in the private sectors of his native homeland and half-a-dozen neighbouring countries. He had dark eyes that obscured his pupils, giving him a deep, penetrating gaze that he focused on Angel as the two men faced off.

'I have been informed of last night's mistake,' Kao said coldly, the way he'd address a subordinate before the handing down of a stiff punishment.

Angel met the other man's stare boldly, letting the liquor catch up with his adrenalin. 'Let me tell you something, Kao,' he retorted, emphasizing his annoyance. 'This isn't Vietnam. You aren't the camp commander any more, and I'm not a POW. You'd do well to remember we're even partners... and this is my country, not yours.'

General Kao's expression remained unchanged. It was as if he hadn't heard a word Angel had said to him. 'You have let Lin Duk Coo slip away,' he said sharply, once Angel had fallen silent. 'You have robbed me of my revenge.'

'We're in the narcotics business, not the revenge business,' Angel reminded Kao testily. 'You have the pipeline from China and I have the distribution network lined up here. I don't see how revenge has anything to do with it.'

Kao issued a condescending sigh, then explained, 'You are not from my culture. Perhaps you should ask your father about the laws of silence... the *omerta* of the American underworld. Perhaps he can explain revenge to you.'

Angel matched Kao's snideness with his own, declaring. 'If you want to get hung up on your outdated codes of honour, that's your problem. I'm concerned about more important things. The people who rescued Coo stole a delivery truck that had the first shipment of "China White" loaded inside it. Two hundred grams, Kao. Ten million dollars. Half of that's yours. If it's discovered, we lose not only the money but our whole distribution plan for transporting the stuff. That's what I'm concerned about, not whether or not you get even with some worthless chef you've got a score with.'

'Lin Duk Coo helped American prisoners to escape from my concentration camp,' General Kao related patiently, his eyes narrowing only slightly. 'I found this out some time ago, but told no one, waiting for the right opportunity to extract my revenge. When I felt the time had come to begin our little enterprise, I sent Lin Duk Coo as my messenger with the understanding that he would be killed once he had performed his task for me. That was to be my revenge for his traitorous acts against me, and I smiled to myself many times thinking how I had arranged it so perfectly. But not as perfectly as I had thought, it seems, because I left the execution in the hands of one who does not appreciate revenge. You have failed me, Lieutenant.'

'Give it a rest, Kao!' Angel snapped heatedly. 'I'm tired of hearing about it, okay?'

'No, it is not okay,' Kao told him. He waited several seconds, holding Angel's gaze, wearing down the other man's resistance until the first glimmer of fear showed itself through the liquor-induced veil of bravado. 'A new distribution network can be set up if need be, but this cook who defied me must die. I want Lin Duk Coo dead.'

'So I've noticed.'

General Kao raised a thin finger and pointed it at Angel's face. 'You will accomplish this or I will fill his grave with your body.'

Without awaiting Angel's response to the threat, the man in the white suit turned and re-entered the helicopter. The pilot worked the throttle and gears, lifting the chopper up and away, stirring the ground with the windy force of its rotors. Angel stood firm and watched the retreating aircraft. It was all he could do to keep from trembling.

SEVEN

When Amy Allen wasn't dabbling in danger with the A-Team, she earned her living as an investigative reporter for the Los Angeles Courier-Express. Her journalistic resources had helped the team on numerous assignments in the past, and she figured that a few hours of research at the paper's morgue might turn up some valuable information regarding the liaison between Tom Angel and General Kao. Reporting to work, she was forced to spend half the day meeting her deadline on a story about a fraudulent art dealer before being able to sneak out of the office to pore over files in the Courier-Express basement. To her pleasant surprise, she unearthed a stack of pertinent newsclippings within the first half-hour. Feeding them to the copying machine, she compiled a dossier she could take out of the building then returned to her office to make a few calls to substantiate and update the material she'd got from the morgue. By the time she returned to the condominium the sun was setting behind her, streaking the cirrus clouds that had gathered over the ocean with swathes of vibrant colour that were reflected on the mirrored surfaces of the twin towers.

Taking the elevator up to the top floor, Amy was halfway down the hallway when she began to hear the muffled sound of boisterous singing. Howling Mad Murdock was living up to his name, crooning like a coyote under the spell of the full moon:

> 'Well, come along boys
> And listen to my tale,
> I'll tell you my troubles
> On the Old Chisolm Trail.

Come a-ti-yi-yippee
Yippee-ay-yippee-ay
Come a-ti-yi-yippee
Yippee-ay.'

Lin Duk Coo was joining Murdock on the chorus, still mired in his inability to belt out more than a strident 'Ay-yi-yi', no matter how hard he tried to get the words right.

As BA went to answer Amy's knock on the door, she could hear him bellow, 'Murdock, I said stop it! Man, you're drivin' me nuts with that singin'!'

BA opened the door a crack to see who it was, then let Amy in.

'Range Rider at it again?' Amy cracked.

BA nodded miserably, shooting Murdock a hard glance. 'And if he keeps it up, I'm gonna drop-kick him all the way back to the range so I won't have to hear him!'

Hannibal was out on the terrace, puffing on a cigar as he enjoyed the sunset with Face. Spotting Amy, the two men came back inside.

'Any luck?' Hannibal asked her.

'I didn't find anything on General Kao,' Amy replied, handing Hannibal the file she'd put together, 'but there's enough on Angel to help put the pieces together, I think.'

'Oh yeah?'

As Hannibal browsed through the clippings, Amy told the others, 'This is going to really get you. His father is Big Rog Angel, an old crime kingpin who's semi-retired now in Arizona. Seems that his boy Tommy changed his name to Anderson as a cover when he took over the bakery operations here five, six years ago. Of course, bread-making's just a front. Word is he's been running his family's dope operation from the bakery since day one, although nobody's been able to hang anything on him.'

'The dope part doesn't surprise me,' Face said. 'Back in 'Nam he did a lot of dealing, even while he was in prison. We figured he got his stash in exchange for finking to Kao.'

'And the stuff Angel peddled was nickel-and-dime compared to what the General was dealin' in,' BA added. 'I'll bet anything that's what's goin' on between 'em now. Some kinda drug scam.'

'What do you think, Lin?' Hannibal asked.

Lin hesitated a moment, then nodded his head bleakly. 'General Kao have fingers in many shady dealings. I try to look other way, but can't help see and hear things.'

'That's probably a big reason why he wanted you killed after he'd got some use out of you,' Hannibal guessed.

'We're going to have to come up with a way to pop their balloon,' Face said. 'I tell ya, I wouldn't mind seeing to it that both Angel and Kao end up in a cell where they throw away the key.'

'What we need is a plan,' Hannibal murmured, still skimming through the newsclippings in the file. 'Hmmmmmm. Amy, you've got the word "golf" scribbled in the margin of this article on Angel's country club membership. Why's that?'

'Apparently he's a real nut on golf,' Amy said. 'I called the club and they say he plays eighteen holes Tuesdays, Thursdays, and Saturdays.'

'Alone?'

Amy shook her head. 'With two other guys. A chauffeur and a bodyguard. The pro at the club says they're both better than Angel but know better than to beat him.'

'Sound pretty loyal to me,' Face said.

'Also sounds like the two goons that nabbed Lin at the restaurant.' Hannibal was grinning slightly now, and his eyes held a glimmer that betrayed the meshing of mental gears.

'I don't like it when he gets that look,' Face grumbled.

Lin Duk Coo smiled. 'The colonel, he love it when plan comes together.'

'He sure does, Lin,' Hannibal remarked, closing the file and tapping ash from his cigar into a coaster on the coffee table. 'He sure does. Tomorrow's Tuesday, isn't it?'

'Sure is,' Amy said.

'Then we've got our work cut out for us,' Hannibal announced.

'What're we doin'?' BA asked.

Hannibal blew a smoke ring and grasped an imaginary golf club as he called out, 'Fore . . .'

EIGHT

The Hillfair Country Club was tucked away in the Hollywood Hills, where it lived up to the difficult challenge of surpassing the opulence of the majority of mansions and estates surrounding its rambling grounds. Meticulously cared for, the golf course was a favourite choice for professionals and celebrities alike, many of whom lived within walking distance of the first tee. Tom Angel lived in Malibu, and there were at least a dozen quality courses closer to his home than Hillfair, but it was here that he came three times a week, for the simple reason that he was able to play the course for a half-dozen strokes lower score than anywhere else he'd tried his luck since moving to Los Angeles. He was also particularly fond of the clubhouse's lunch menu, and he invariably spent two hours between his rounds of golf dining and doing business over a phone brought to his table.

Aside from his basic enjoyment of the game, Angel played golf as a way of keeping in shape and working off stress, but today he had too much on his mind to be soothed by the pursuit of the little white ball across the rolling fields of green. He'd played a terrible first nine, racking up his worst score since first joining the club, and to make matters worse, the kitchen had been out of fresh shrimp, forcing him to bypass his usual lunch offering in favour of a French Dip sandwich that seemed to settle in the pit of his stomach like bits of training weights. General Kao's warning hung over him like a dark pall, troubling his thoughts and making concerns over his golf game and the viscosity of the *au jus* sauce seem insignificant in comparison.

'All right, let's go get the last nine out of the way,' he said after scribbling his signature on the cheque. His chauffeur and his bodyguard, both men dressed in designer togs from the pro shop next door, silently complied, rising from the table and heading out the door leading to the tenth hole.

Three middle-aged men in tacky outfits of madras and polyester were sitting near the tee, trading jokes as they looked over the clubs they'd be toting for Angel and his cohorts.

'... and so I says, "I'd bet my wife on it",' one of the grey-haired caddies chortled in anticipation of his punchline. 'And he says, "Your wife? I was kinda hopin' you'd put up yer dog!"'

As the other two caddies looked at one another to make sure they hadn't missed something, the man who had told the joke supplied his own laughtrack, guffawing so hard that he almost shook loose the false moustache and make-up concealing his true identity, that of Hannibal Smith.

'Who are you?' Angel demanded, eyeing Hannibal sternly. 'Where's Melville?'

'He took ill while you were to lunch, sah,' Hannibal explained.

'Ill? He seemed all right to me when he was caddying the first nine.'

'Come on kinda sudden-like, I guess,' Hannibal drawled. 'Anyhow, Melville said mebbe I could bring you a spot of good luck for a change, though I don't claim to know what he's talkin' about, sah...'

'Never mind the voodoo... what's your name?'

'Eugene. But friends call me Genie, on account of my bringin' good luck,' Hannibal said, pulling out a driver from Angel's bag. 'Here you go, sah. You'll be happy with Genie, I kin promise ya.'

'Yeah, well, I like a caddy who knows when to shut up!' Angel snapped as he took the club from Hannibal and went over to tee off.

As he looked on, Hannibal took a few steps back, joining the other caddies.

'Genie, huh?' one of them remarked dubiously. 'We'll see

about that. Mister Angel's been colder than a witch's mitt all day.'

The entire group fell silent as Angel propped a ball on his tee and took a few practice swings, then proceeded to clobber the ball a good two hundred and fifty yards down the centre of the fairway.

'I'll be damned,' he muttered aloud.

'Nice shot, sir,' his bodyguard told him.

Hannibal beamed as he took the driver back from Angel. 'You got good wood on that one, sah. Yes indeedy.'

'Yeah, I did, didn't I?' Angel grinned for the first time all day. 'Maybe you're good luck for me after all.'

'Like they say, sah, you ain't seen nothin' yet,' Hannibal promised, not bothering to mention that he'd slipped Angel a supply of doctored golf balls while he was at lunch. Mother Teresa could have teed off for a good distance with the ball Angel had hit.

Angel had both a page beeper and a portable phone clipped to his belt, and while the other two men were teeing off, he wandered off near the ball-washers and put through a quick call to the bakery, checking to see if there was any news on the search for Lin Duk Coo. Hannibal wasn't close enough to overhear the conversation, but from the wealth of expletives Angel spewed after clamping the phone back on his waist, he presumed that none of the golfer's goons had fallen back onto Lin's scent, or Hannibal's for that matter.

The chauffeur and the bodyguard shot a hook and slice, respectively, landing both balls well shy of Angel's drive. They required second shots just to catch up with Angel and reach a part of the fairway affording a glimpse of the green, which was surrounded by woods and sand traps. As the group gathered around Angel for his three iron shot, they noticed two men lingering on the green, apparently more interested in carrying on a conversation than putting out and moving on to the next hole.

'Come on, you guys!' Angel screamed out to them, anxious to see if his second shot would be as good as his first. 'We're waiting out here. Putt, will ya?'

When the duo on the green continued to idle near the pin,

50

Hannibal said, 'They either don't hear you or don't want to hear you, sah. That'd be my guess.'

'Doesn't take much to see that,' Angel responded hotly. Turning to his sidekicks, he said, 'Don, Solly, go up there and get those guys moving, will ya? If I'm on a roll, I don't want to lose it.'

The chauffeur and bodyguard handed their clubs back to their caddies and headed purposefully towards the distant green, where Templeton Peck and Howling Mad Murdock, dressed like spoiled heirs, continued to do everything but putt. Peck was lining up his shot with every possible technique short of lugging out a computer to calculate the many variables to be taken into consideration when making a seven-inch putt. Murdock, on the other hand, was down on one knee, looking as if he were genuflecting in the presence of an alien being who had chosen to come to earth in the form of a Topflight Turfmaster.

'I'm telling you, Face, my ball can talk,' Murdock insisted. 'It can, it really can.'

'Right, Murdock, and my putter knows how to tap-dance to Dixieland music.'

Murdock plucked up his ball, which had a sliced cut across its facing so that it bore a faint resemblance to the cheerful mug that spent most of the seventies telling people to 'Have a Nice Day'. 'Say something nice to the Faceman,' Murdock asked the ball.

'Lots of them can talk,' Face conceded, noticing Angel's brutes stepping up onto the green out of the corner of his eye. 'But can it sing?'

'I haven't taught it any songs yet,' Murdock responded quickly. 'Good idea, though, Face.'

Murdock was halfway through the first stanza of 'The Old Chisolm Trail' when he and Face were confronted by four hundred and fifty pounds of potential violence.

'You guys wanna get off the green?' Don, the bodyguard asked with restrained politeness. 'Mr Anderson is waiting to hit his ball up here.'

Murdock clucked his tongue at his ball. 'Company coming, and you with nothing to wear. Tsk, tsk.'

'Really funny, guys,' Solly deadpanned, cracking his knuckles loud enough to give Peck and Murdock the idea their bones could make the same sound in his hands.

'Well, if you don't like the jokes, then let's try some business.' Peck had managed to position himself so that his back was turned to the fairway. He'd been wearing baggy pants, the better to conceal a .38 revolver in his front pocket. He jerked it out and held it close to his side so that Angel couldn't see him from behind. Don and Solly saw the gun, and they didn't like the idea of it pointing at them.

'Hey, ace, I already know what the score of one of –'

'Shut up and just stand where you are. If Angel, or Anderson... whatever you want to call him, if he gets suspicious, I'm giving each of you a hole in one, right where it counts.'

The gun was pointed at a part of Don's anatomy not normally associated with counting. Don had no plans to raise a family, but he was fond of his jewels and he didn't care to risk the chance of losing any part of the collection. Both he and Solly stayed put, trying not to look back at their boss.

Pacing around his ball, Angel glared at the green. 'What's their problem up there?' He raised his voice and shouted, 'Come on, Don! Get those bums off the green and get back here so we can play through!'

Hannibal unslung his golf bag and pulled the knitted slipcover off what was supposed to be a two iron but was instead an A.R.-15 rifle. In the time it took for Angel to realize what had just happened, Hannibal pulled the weapon out into the open and tested to make sure it worked. It did, sending a few bursts pummelling into the turf near Angel's Gucci-clad feet.

'I'm sure you've got a popgun on you somewhere, friend,' Hannibal said. 'Take it out slowly and drop it.'

The other two caddies shrank back in fear as Angel reached into his pocket and pulled out a small .22, which he held by the barrel as he stared at Hannibal. 'Who are you?'

'I told you to drop it.' Once Angel had complied, Hannibal reached up to his face and pried off the false moustache and make-up as he said, 'So, how you been, Lieutenant? Still selling other people's stuff . . . just like in 'Nam?'

Once Angel had a face to place alongside Hannibal's voice, he was able to dredge up the right memories and know who he was facing. 'Colonel? Colonel Smith?'

'At your disservice.' Keeping the rifle trained on Angel, Hannibal reached into one of the side pockets of his golf bag for a walkie-talkie. Bringing it to his lips, he signalled, 'We're ready.'

An engine came to life in the woods, and BA burst out into the open in his van, clearing the rough and rolling out onto the green near where Hannibal was holding Angel captive. Face and Murdock led Don and Solly over as Amy emerged from the rear of the van and held the doors open.

'In you go, all three of you,' Hannibal announced to Angel and his goons. 'We're gonna have a pow-wow.'

'You don't know what you're messing with, Smith,' Angel advised, refusing to move.

'Sure I do,' Hannibal shot back, 'but I'm impetuous. I'm also nuts and trigger-happy. Get in the van before I foam at the mouth and start blasting.'

Don and Solly weren't about to call Hannibal's bluff. They climbed into the van without hesitation, with Peck keeping them covered with his .38. Angel finally broke down and followed.

'Smart thinking, Angel,' Hannibal told him. 'Now let's get away from the links and go someplace where we can have a little privacy . . .'

NINE

As BA drove further up into the hills, there was an uneasy silence in the back of the van. The three prisoners were determined not to talk or cooperate any further on their abduction. They sat and stared with stony malice at Hannibal and Peck, who kept them under armed guard. Murdock was in the back, too, wiping smudges of dirt and grass-stains off his pet golfball. He noticed Don watching him and went into another ventriloquist's act, using the ball as his dummy.

'You think we like getting socked around the course all day long?' the ball seemed to be whining in a high-pitched voice. 'Well, we don't. This is just a warning from the Golfball Liberation Army... let my people be!'

Don looked at Murdock, then Solly, then Hannibal. 'Is that it?' he demanded. 'You're taking us hostage because we hit golfballs?'

'Guess again, bicep-brain,' Hannibal taunted. 'Don't pretend you don't recognize us from the restaurant and the bakery. You know why we're going on a cruise.'

'Don, shut up,' Angel told his bodyguard. 'If anybody talks to these misfits, it'll be me.'

'How nice,' Hannibal said. 'I always like to take my complaints to the man in charge. Hey, BA, how we doin'?'

'Comin' up, Hannibal.'

At the top of the hill, there was an undeveloped parcel of land, overgrown with weeds and bottlebrush. With a little landscaping and the right sales-pitch, the plot would sell for a cool million a few months down the line. Until then, it would continue to be used as a playground for neighbourhood children and a make-out mecca for the local adolescents. BA pulled off the main road and followed two ruts back into the thick of the brush, beyond the view of neighbouring residences. Once the van had stopped, Murdock opened the rear doors slightly and struck out his arm with the golfball in his hand. The white orb seemed to check the vicinity with the thoroughness of a cartoon periscope, then piped out, 'All clear . . .'

The rear doors opened all the way and Murdock scrambled out, followed by the prisoners, Hannibal, and Peck. Amy and BA got out of the front and came around to join the others.

'Face, Amy, take the lookout,' Hannibal ordered.

Peck handed Murdock his gun, then grabbed the A-Team's vintage Thompson submachine gun from the back of the van and headed back the way they'd come. Amy unslung the binoculars from around her neck and started up a knoll that would give her a fairly unobstructed view of the area. As Hannibal finished shedding the rest of his caddie disguise, Anderson folded his hands across his chest. 'Okay, very neat, Colonel,' he said. 'You always did have a flair for unusual plans. Let's say I'm impressed.'

'Let's say you're in trouble.' Hannibal gestured to a spot several yards away. 'Why don't you step over there, away from your boyfriends.'

Angel needed a prod in the ribs from Murdock's gun to get moving. 'You guys are the ones in trouble,' he advised Hannibal, clinging to his last shred of bravado. 'I guess you've found out who my father is.'

'Yeah, big dope dealer. Perfect guy to breed a little dope like you, Tommy. Only problem is, your daddy's a long ways from here. You could cry and he wouldn't hear you.' Hannibal paused to light up a cigar, then shook out the match and tossed it good-naturedly at Angel, leaving a nick of ash on the dealer's white shirt. 'Lemme tell you how we see things, Angel. General Kao was into drug peddling back before it became fashionable, and he had a good thing going as vice-king of the Orient. When the US started messing around in 'Nam, he figured it was time to expand his operations, find a way to get his junk into the states. Ten years ago, along comes Big Rog Angel's little boy Tommy. He ends up in the General's POW camp and – *voila!* – Kao's got the perfect solution to his distribution problem. He stroked you and you sold out, right, kid? The rest of the prisoners are eatin' cockroaches and grass while you're in General Kao's headquarters, dining on smoked oysters and having your nails buffed while you lay plans for a few years down the road.'

'That was ten years ago,' Angel countered, a trace of urgency in his voice. 'Even you can't carry a grudge that long.'

'Lotta guys died there, man!' BA shouted, taking a step forward and giving Angel a slight shove. Angel backpedalled past the bottlebrush, moving out of sight of his henchmen, who Murdock continued to hold at bay. 'Lotta guys died and you coulda helped 'em!' BA went on, his rage building. 'You had the leverage, but you didn't do nothing!'

'So we square it for them right now. We drop you in a hole and all debts are paid,' Hannibal said.

'Hey, lighten up, Colonel,' Angel laughed nervously. 'Don't you think you're getting a little carried away here?'

'I don't think so, Lieutenant.' Hannibal stepped forward and gave Angel a second shove. This time, when the golfer reeled backwards, the ground gave way beneath him and he let out a shriek of terror as he fell into an open grave. Landing roughly on the dirt bottom, he sprained an ankle and groaned from the pain. As he tried to get to his feet, Hannibal told him, 'Try kneeling, Angel. It's time to say your prayers.'

Angel looked up and saw Hannibal pointing the automatic rifle at him. 'Somebody'll hear if you shoot,' he babbled desperately. 'You won't get away with it.'

Hannibal patted his weapon. 'It'll sound like firecrackers or a jackhammer. Nobody'll think twice about it, except for your goons. We'll probably have to change their nappies before we throw them in on top of you.'

Angel's mind was racing, trying to think his way out of his dilemma. He decided to opt for the criminal's favourite means of persuasion: bribery. 'You gotta be a better businessman than that, Colonel. I know about you guys. I read the papers. You're hot... the bad kinda hot. You could use money, right? Maybe we can make a deal...'

'I'm not for sale,' Hannibal retorted.

'Everybody's for sale, Colonel,' Angel insisted. 'It's one of the few constants in life. It's just a matter of hitting the right place.'

'You really believe that, don't you, sucker!?' BA said, kicking dirt down on Angel. 'Forget it, man!'

Angel pretended he hadn't heard BA. Shaking dirt from his hair, he eyed Hannibal and bartered, 'You've got my bakery truck and you've got Lin Duk Coo. I need both of them. I'm willing to pay one million dollars cash if you turn them over to me.'

'No deal.' Hannibal, however, seemed to open up to the idea of negotiation. He lowered his rifle and flicked cigar ash at Angel. 'You're gonna have to come up with something a little more substantial.'

Angel brightened slightly. 'Like what?'

'Not what. Who. I want General Kao.'

Angel stiffened, sucking in his breath. 'He's not even in this country,' he lied.

'Lin says he's here,' Hannibal countered. 'Look, Lieutenant, there's all kinda ways to get dope outta the Orient. The General is just one of them. You don't need him. You're a smart kid. You'll come up with another supplier.'

'What are you getting at?'

'I already told you. I want Kao. I can't get your nails buffed for you, Tommy, but I could keep you alive. Think about it.'

'I can't when I'm stuck down in this hole,' Angel snapped. 'You gotta give me some time. I need to call my father.'

'You got four hours. Give us a number.'

Angel reached for his wallet and pulled out a business card, which he handed to Hannibal. 'It's my office at the bakery. There's a number on the back too. That's for this phone on my belt.'

'Good. Remember, four hours.'

BA and Hannibal turned and walked off, leaving Angel in the hole. He called out, 'You're gonna let me walk, huh? Just like that? What if I double-cross you?'

Hannibal stopped and looked back at Angel. 'Hey, kiddo, you aren't that swift. I did some pretty squirrelly stuff back in 'Nam and lived to talk about it. I've done all right since I got back to the states, too. To me, you're just bread on a windowsill, mine whenever I want you. The only thing saving you is I want the General more.'

BA and Hannibal headed off around the bottlebrush, coming up to where Murdock had managed to link Don and Solly to each other with a pair of handcuffs. Don's hands were connected to Solly's wrists, and vice-versa, so that they looked like human pretzels sprawled out on the grass.

'Viva la golfball!' Murdock shouted triumphantly, chalking up a victory for his oppressed companion.

'Nice job, Murdock,' Hannibal said, admiring his associate's handiwork. 'Now let's get outta here...'

TEN

'Shut up, fool! I can't pull this muffler off with you jibber-jabberin' in my ear!'

BA rolled out from under the bakery truck and waved a crescent wrench in Murdock's face for emphasis. Murdock was sitting on the back bumper, hopelessly mired in the depths of melancholy, staring tragically at the golfball in his hand as if it were Yorick's skull. His mournful soliloquy, however, was far from Shakespeare.

'Sure ... sure,' he sniffed, his voice trembling, 'You live in a nice hotel. How would you like to be stuffed in the side pocket of a golf bag, along with half-chewed pencils and old tees that were still caked with dirt?'

'How would you like it if I tossed that damn ball down the sewer and used this wrench to rearrange your vocal chords, sucker!'

Murdock cupped both hands over the ball, hiding it from view. He offered BA an apologetic smile.

'Man, nobody can accuse us of not hirin' the handicapped,' BA grumbled as he slid back under the truck and applied more elbow pressure to the obstinate nut keeping the muffler still attached to the chassis.

'BA?' Murdock whispered softly, testing to see if Baracus could hear him. When there was no response from under the truck, Murdock uncupped one hand from over the golfball and slowly began to pet it. He started talking to the ball in the same low voice, but as he became increasingly swept up by his emotion, he spoke louder. 'Hairy fingers pull you out, make you stand on your tippy-toes on top of that dirty tee ... you, not even fully awake yet ... and then ... then they take

59

out a club... a club... and they stand over you and you close your little eyes while they wind up... and swing that club with all their might, hitting you in your little face, driving you off that tee with so much force...'

Murdock was so caught up in his pathos that he didn't see BA re-emerge from beneath the truck, muffler in hand. BA grabbed Murdock by the collar of his shirt and brought their faces close together. 'It's a golfball, idiot! It's nothin' but a golf ball! You're drivin' me nuts, man! Look, you see this?' He held out the muffler for Murdock to see. 'One more word and I'll use this like a baseball bat to smack that ball so hard it'll wish it never left the factory. You got that?'

Inside the truck, Lin Duk Coo and Amy were standing near the bread racks, slicing each loaf down the middle as if preparing submarine sandwiches. Watching BA and Murdock, Lin smirked, 'Nothing changes.'

'That's for sure,' Amy agreed. 'Those two go together like oil and water.'

'Like Laurel and Hardy, I think,' Lin said. 'Even in prison camp, they were always good for a laugh.'

'What was the camp like?' Amy asked, her journalistic instincts taking over. 'Those guys never seem to want to talk too much about it.'

'Very bad times,' Lin said. 'Maybe they not want to talk about it because it wakes up the memory. Is best to forget how badly men can treat each other.'

'All I know is I've never seen Hannibal so fired up to settle an old score. He wants to get his hands on General Kao in the worst way.'

'As bad as Hannibal wants Kao, Kao wants me,' Lin said, shivering at the thought. 'I plenty lucky to be rescued by A-Team before General gets hands on me, or maybe I end up like human sushi for him to feed to his pigs.'

The garage elevator opened and Hannibal stepped out, followed by Peck.

'How's it going?' Hannibal asked as he came over. 'Find anything?'

As the others shook their heads, BA pleaded, 'Take this fool back with you, okay, Colonel? I can't take much more of this golfball liberation stuff.'

'Well, BA, you talk to your tools sometimes,' Murdock sniffed defensively. 'And I can't even bear to repeat some of the things you've said to them.'

'See what I mean?' BA said. 'He's been outta the hatch for too long. I say we oughta call off his furlough and ship him back to the vet's hospital. Let some shrink listen to him gabbin' with his ball, not me!'

Hannibal surveyed the various parts that BA had already removed from the truck. Besides the muffler, he'd pulled out the inner panels, popped the hubcaps, and dismantled half of the engine compartment. Hannibal picked up the air filter and shook it a few times, then set it back down, murmuring, 'There's gotta be something valuable on this truck.'

As BA went to work on disconnecting the rear bumper, Face exclaimed, 'Hey, BA, you're strewing stuff all over the floor here!'

'Where you expect me to strew it?' BA said.

'Look, we have a maintenance policy in this building,' Peck complained. 'You're not supposed to mess the common areas, and the garage is a common area.'

'I'll mess what I wanna mess, man.' As if to prove it, BA dropped the loosened bumper on the concrete, sending caked dirt and grime flying. Face stepped back just in time to keep from having his white slacks tarnished.

'Next time we choose a hideout, count me out,' Peck told Hannibal. 'I'm tired of having my good things spoiled by Attila and his Happy Huns.'

Amy called out from inside the truck, 'Hannibal, what makes you so sure there's something in here anyway?'

'Angel was gonna pay us a million dollars for this truck and Lin Duk Coo. That stirred my curiosity.' Hannibal reached for a loaf of bread and broke it in half, checking the inside. 'My guess is there's some "China White" stuffed away in some hidey-hole here.'

'I remember that movie, too!' Murdock shouted excitedly. 'Popeye Doyle, stripping that poor limo down to the bare bones trying to get a bead on the French Connection. Man, we could turn this into a sequel!'

'There's already been a sequel,' Peck reminded him.

'A trequel then!' Murdock's eyes began to dazzle from the supposed glow of an imaginary marquee. 'The China Connection 3-D, with Odorama! Help sniff out the villains yourself! Starring yours truly as Brutus Doyle, Popeye's long-lost cousin and ace sleuth for Interpol...'

As Murdock continued to pitch his envisioned 'smella-vision' masterpiece, a Mercedes pulled into the parking space next to the truck, and out stepped a dazzling redhead in a black cocktail dress and spiked heels. She gave her head a reflective shake as she stared at the strange tableau before her. The sight of men with dirty hands horrified her.

'Mr Toney, what on earth is going on?'

Peck quickly strode forward, pausing directly in front of the woman in a feeble attempt to block her view of BA's handiwork. 'I... uh... I was planning a little *merci soire* for the folks in the building,' he stammered. 'You know, coffee and cakes in the model. Sort of a thankyou for all the business they've given to Mr Toney Interiors during the last three months. This fella's bakery truck broke down while he was delivering my order.'

'That's all very well and good, Mr Toney,' the redhead replied snootily, 'but this is a common area.'

'I know, I know, I know,' Face said. 'I feel just awful, but accidents will happen, Stella darling...'

Stella was only partially appeased by Peck's explanation, and even less so by his trumped-up display of practised charm. Heading for the elevators, she told Peck, 'Well, you better get it cleared up before Mr Yerkovitch sees it.'

'I will,' Face said, waving. 'Ciao, love.'

Stella stepped into the waiting elevator and turned around, offering a stiff smile to the alleged Mr Toney. 'Ciao...'

As the elevator doors closed and Stella was spirited up to her room on the eighth floor, Peck turned on his companions. 'What have I ever done to you guys, huh? You're gonna get me thrown outta here, and this is the best deal I ever promoted... or at least right up there in the top ten.'

'You never got around to telling us how you worked this scam, Face,' Amy reminded him as she started in on another rack of bread. 'I'm curious.'

'Mr Toney's in Europe for four months. He's never around. I just dropped by one day to see the model and I ... well, I sorta never left.' Peck grinned as he recalled it all. 'The first time I got caught inside the condo, they thought I was Mr Toney. I didn't want to disappoint them, so I played along, and now here we are. Hey, it was just a case of mistaken identity.'

'Hmmmmmmm.' Hannibal reached into his pocket and pulled out a business card. 'So, tell me, Face, did you run these off before or after people started calling you Mr Toney?'

The business card had Peck's picture on it and claimed he was indeed Mr Toney and that he 'invites you to a penthouse decorated in breathless splendour.' Peck blushed as he took the card. 'Well, you know how it goes. When opportunity knocks...'

'"Breathless splendour"?'

'That's decorator talk,' Face explained, clapping his hands like a coach trying to inspire his team at halftime. 'Come on, gang, can we pick up this mess, please? I'd help, but there's a few things I have to check on upstairs.'

'Oh yeah?' Hannibal remarked. 'We were just up there.'

'I know, but it slipped my mind before. You see, I've got a couple dropping by the bar to pay a deposit for a job I'm going to do for them next month.'

'You can't be serious,' Amy said. 'Face, you couldn't decorate an Easter egg without botching things up.'

'I subcontract,' Face told her. 'Okay, look, if I pull off this deposit, I'll buy supper for the whole bunch of you, provided that truck's ready to roll outta here by sundown.'

'That might be too soon,' Hannibal said. 'How about giving us till eight, then buying dessert?'

'You're on.'

'While you're up there, try giving Angel another call and see if he's dredged up General Kao yet.'

'Will do.' Face left the others to their demolition and got

into the elevator. Instead of pushing for the top floor, he pressed the ground level button and rode up, whistling to himself. Getting out one floor up, Face proceeded into the cocktail lounge, where he loaded up a tray of happy hour *hors-d'oeuvres* and quickly devoured them along with a draft beer while he waited for the arrival of his prospective clients. As it turned out, the couple he'd expected showed up with still another couple, and for the next hour Peck was hard-pressed to bluff sufficient expertise to secure a few thousand dollars from both parties, who seemed to feel their destinies in life would be achieved only when their homes had made the pages of House and Garden and that the Mr Toney touch was their best chance of success.

Once he'd sent away the foursome with promises that he would give their homes priority after the first of the month, Peck ordered cognac to toast his own small success, then took his drink to the bar, where he'd spotted a winsome brunette sitting by herself. Before he had a chance to take a seat next to her and launch into his well-rehearsed manoeuvres of seduction, though, someone tapped him on the shoulder from behind. He turned around to face a tall, gaunt man in a dark suit and matching mood.

'Why, Mr Yerkovitch!' Peck greeted the building superintendent with exaggerated enthusiasm. 'What a pleasure.'

'I wish I could say the same,' Yerkovitch rejoined gruffly. 'I just finished talking with Stella Clerkwell up on the eighth floor. Seems you've got a truck in your parking space downstairs that looks like it's being used for vandal lessons by a crew of non-residents. What gives, Mr Toney?'

'They're mechanics, Mr Yerkovitch,' Face explained, staring over the superintendant's shoulder at the brunette, who was paying her bill and getting up to leave. She glanced over at him and smiled seductively, then headed for the exit.

'Mr Toney?' Yerkovitch interupted. 'You were saying...?'

'Yes, yes, forgive me.' Face set his drink down on the bar so he could better lend some body language to his fast talking. 'Of course, I've been on those people like flock on wallpaper, but with these trade types nothing seems to work.

64

They walk to the beat of a different drummer, I'm telling you. I mean, I want to throw a little "Thanks For Being My Friend Party"... a little champagne, Beluga Caviare, and a few pastries... and what do I end up with but a band of Mormons doing exploratory surgery on their truck. I'm mortified by the whole affair, believe me, Mr Yerkovitch.'

'I don't suppose I have to remind you that the garage is a common area, Mr Toney. I've already had five complaints. If you weren't so popular with everyone in this building, I'd be forced to take very strong action. But the complaining tenants didn't want me to do that to you, so I'm hoping a mere warning will suffice.'

Peck signalled for the bartender to pour Yerkovitch a cognac, then patted the super's shoulder reassuringly. 'Well, I can promise I'll have that mess cleaned up by sundown, and I'll have those monsters out of here once and for all.'

'That would be excellent... what's this now?' Yerkovitch glanced down at the drink the bartender had sat next to Peck's.

'I thought we'd share a quick toast before I go,' Peck said, raising his snifter. 'After all, you have a birthday tomorrow, right?'

'How did you know that?' Yerkovitch said, genuinely impressed.

Staring out the front doors, Peck saw the mysterious brunette standing by the kerb, trying to flag down a taxi. He turned his attention back to Yerkovitch and quickly chinked his snifter against the other man's. 'It's not important. What counts is that a man needs to start out another year on the right foot. Cheers.'

'Why, thank you, Mr Toney.'

Peck drained the rest of his cognac, then licked his lips as he set the empty snifter back on the bar. 'Well, I must be going, sir. Don't worry, I'l take care of that truck.'

'No hurry,' Yerkovitch told him. 'By morning would do.'

'You got it.' Peck turned on his heels and paced quickly out the door, just as the brunette was getting into a taxi. 'Wait!' he shouted, rushing up to her.

'Yes?' she chirped merrily, rolling down the back window.

65

'Look, I don't have time to bore you with my usual routine right this minute,' he told her, deciding to forsake subtlety in favour of directness. 'I think we should get together some time soon.'

'How about tonight?' the woman responded.

'Tonight?' Peck gasped, taken by surprise. 'Tonight! Sure. Great, why not?'

'I can't think of any reason,' she cooed. 'I'm staying with my girlfriend in number nine. I'll be back in a few hours. Why don't you stop by and pick me up?'

'Anywhere special you'd like to go?'

'How about your place?'

'My place... fine, yes, of course,' Peck babbled. 'No transportation hassles that way.'

'See you then,' the woman said, rolling up her window as the cabbie pulled away from the kerb. Before she was driven out of sight, she called out, 'My name's Gayle.'

'I'm Toney... Mr... I mean, Dr Tony Cork. I work on brains. I'll stop by at eight!' Peck shouted at the retreating cab. Once the vehicle rounded a corner, he floated back inside and pushed the down button for an elevator. '"Dr Tony Cork. I work on brains"? Oh, Peck, you are a real smoothie. Where do you come up with them?' he muttered to himself.

Peck's buoyant spirits were promptly punctured when he stepped out of the elevator downstairs and took one look at the truck. Instead of being reassembled, the vehicle had been broken down into twice as many separate parts as the last time he'd seen it, and the others were chipping in with BA to speed up the dismantling.

'What're you doing?' Face shrieked, coming out of his romantic daydreaming as he hurried over to the scene of destruction taking place in Mr Toney's parking place. 'We've got to get all this cleaned up! Now!'

Hannibal also had an other-worldly look on his face, but it was due to more pressing concerns than the prospects of a lover's tryst. 'I'm telling you, it's here somewhere!' he seethed, slitting open a sun vizor and running his fingers through the cotton padding in the hope of finding the elusive

66

drugs he suspected were concealed in the truck.

'That was kinda fun,' Amy said, wiping sweat from her brow with the sleeve of her blouse. 'I've never ripped apart forty loaves of bread before. And to think I went unfulfilled for so long.'

'Very funny, Amy, Hannibal told her.

As Lin Duk Coo helped Murdock haul the emptied bread rack out of the truck, Amy moved over and sat down on a pallet that had inadvertently been set on top of several loaves of unchecked bread. The pressure of her weight on the pallet was enough to make the loaves pop and shoot out a powdery white cloud from their ruptured ends. Amy jumped up with surprise and the others looked at the source of the noise.

'Either those loaves are undercooked, or Amy found the stash,' Murdock said, moving over to raise the pallet from the suspicious bread. As he and Amy started carefully prying open the other loaves stacked there, Hannibal dabbed his finger into some of the white powder and tasted it.

'Hello, hello,' he said. 'It's heroin, all right.'

'And there's plenty more where that came from,' Amy said, pulling plastic bags from other loaves that were filled with more of the powder.

'I think we find jackpot,' Lin Duk Coo declared.

ELEVEN

Tom Angel pulled out his cigarettes and realized there was only one left in the pack. He put it in his mouth and crumpled the pack into a ball, wishing he could do the same to Hannibal Smith, Lin Duk Coo, General Kao and all the other people responsible for his miseries of the past few days. He couldn't remember the last time he'd been subjected to so much harassment and indignity, unless it had been back in 'Nam, during the first few weeks in the POW camp, before he'd befriended Kao and wrangled himself a privileged status amongst the prisoners. At least it wouldn't last for long, he told himself as he lit the cigarette. After a few days of taut nerves and insomnia, he figured he'd have the dirt in his life swept under the carpet and would emerge from the experience in better shape than he'd been in going into it. Once he'd got the truck and Lin Duk Coo back, he'd get rid of Hannibal's ragtag commandos, mend fences with General Kao, and get the heroin distribution system working to the point where he could take some time off. The yachting season was getting underway on the East Coast, and he was determined that once he'd skimmed off his profits from the first shipment of 'China White', he'd fly to New York, buy himself a sixty-footer and spend a few weeks lazing on the Atlantic, dining on the world's best seafood and rubbing elbows with Old Wealth. Maybe he'd be able to scout up some action around Atlantic City to get involved with that might help turn him into a bi-coastal sort of guy. Big plans, big plans. But there were matters to tend to in the meantime.

'Don't you guys have that damn thing rigged up yet?' he snapped, staring across his office at Don and Solly, who were labouring on either side of Angel's phone, rigging up a recording device and several other pieces of equipment to it.

'Almost there, boss,' Solly said.

'Well, speed it up. If the call comes through before we're finished, it'll all be a waste of time.' Angel took a long drag on his cigarette, then got up from his desk. 'I'm going down the hall for some more smokes. I want that system ready to go when I get back!'

It was the middle of a hectic workday, and the hallway outside Angel's office was bustling with activity. If it weren't for the fact that Angel was greedy and criminal by nature, he would have had no problems earning an honest living just off the profits of the bread company, which had been operating in the black for most of the past decade. The bakery's output was large enough to satisfy consumer demand throughout the entire state, and it was through use of his fleet of delivery trucks that Angel planned to expand his heroin distribution network.

After pausing to dispense a few orders to his crew foremen, Angel continued down the hall to the bank of vending machines that provided workers with everything from breath mints to burgers. He fed a few quarters to the cigarette machine and pulled for his brand. As the pack tumbled down the chute for him to pick up, Angel sensed that he was not alone.

'Do you have Lin Duk Coo for me yet?' an unmistakable voice called out behind him. Angel turned and saw General Kao standing in the doorway, dressed the same as he had been during their last confrontation.

'I'm working on it!' Angel dropped what was left of his last cigarette and ground it underfoot as he opened a fresh pack.

'I heard you shouting at men in your office becuse they were so slow in doing their jobs,' General Kao replied. 'Perhaps I should shout at you in the hope of getting results.'

'I'll get you your damn results,' Angel yelled. 'I don't need you shouting, and I don't need you snooping around my office like some two-bit spy. Now get the hell out of here before you blow my cover! I know where to reach you, and once I have Lin Duk Coo, I'll leave him on your doorstep.

Understood?'

General Kao nodded his head imperceptibly. 'I will give you until this time tomorrow.'

'How white of you, General. And what happens if I don't have him by then?'

'You do not wish to find out,' Kao informed Angel. 'Trust me on that.'

The general turned and walked out the door, only a few seconds before Solly shouted down the hallway from Angel's office, 'Phone's for you, boss!'

Angel hurried back to his office, his heart racing. Once inside, he closed the door and whispered to Don, 'General Kao just left through the side door. I want him followed and I want to know where he is every second so we can use him for trade bait.' After Don had slipped out the door, Angel looked over at Solly, who was manning their equipment linked up to the phone. Solly gave a thumbs-up sign and Angel could see that the recorder was already taping. He picked up the phone. 'Yeah?'

'Smith here,' Hannibal told him. 'Not bad, Tom. Little plastic baggies of skag inside the bread . . . that's real clever. Good way to ship it around the country. Gives new meaning to the phrase "Wonder Bread". "Builds wrong minds twelve different ways", eh?'

'You calling to swap puns, Colonel?' Angel asked. 'Maybe you should try Johnny Carson.'

'It's not puns I want to swap, Lieutenant. I figure we've got a million dollars in heroin here, more or less, depending on how much you've cut it. Here's the deal. You have the General meet us at Indian Dunes, noon tomorrow.'

'How am I supposed to get him there?'

'Tell him we've got Lin Duk Coo. That should bring him running. We trade even up, the dope and Lin for General Kao. No draft picks, no players to be named later.'

Angel mulled it over a moment, lighting up his cigarette and staring over at Solly, who was feverishly toying with a console filled with buttons and dials that would hopefully be able to trace where Hannibal was calling from.

'Stall him,' Solly whispered to Angel. 'I need more time.'

Over the phone, Hannibal said, 'You say something, Angel?'

'I'm not sure I can deliver,' Angel said. 'Can I put you on hold a second while I call Kao on the other phone? Then I can let you know right off if I can get –'

'No way, Tommy ol' boy. You'll deliver, period. After all, we're not talking bread sticks here ... we're talking millions in heroin and your entire distribution setup, not to mention a good twenty years upriver if we hang a trafficking rap on you.'

'Now, wait a minute, Smith. I don't... hello?' Angel pulled the receiver away from his ear. 'Damn it, he hung up!'

Before Angel could hang up on his end, Solly lunged over and grabbed the receiver from him saying, 'We've still got one chance left!'

Solly brought the receiver to his ear and waited, at the same time disconnecting the other equipment.

'How's that supposed to work?' Angel demanded.

'You'll find out, provided their call went out through a switchboard.'

'What?'

'Shhhhhh.'

After a few seconds, the voice of an operator sounded in Solly's ear. 'If you're through with this call, please hang up.'

'This is the telephone company,' Solly said in an officious voice. 'Time and charges on that last call ... fifteen sixty-five for sixteen message units.'

'This is the switchboard at Century Towers West,' the operator replied. 'Recontact your party for those charges, please.'

Solly hung up the phone and grinned at Angel. 'We got lucky. They're in the Century Towers West. I think it's a condo high-rise.'

'I know the place,' Angel said. 'Good work. Now that we know where they are, I think it's time we paid them back for that little stunt they pulled on us back on the golf course.'

'Man, I'm all for that. Let's do it now.'

Angel shook his head. 'I think they'd be too much on their guard. Let's wait awhile. Let 'em think they've got us over a barrel for a few hours, then they'll get lax and we'll make our move . . .'

TWELVE

The penthouse kitchen smelled like a miniature bakery, and when Lin Duk Coo removed another tray of golden loaves from the oven, their tantalizing aroma wafted through the entire condominium. The kitchen table was already filled with loaves made over the past hours, so Lin took the rack over to the counter, where Amy was stirring up a new batch of dough.

'Those look wonderful, Lin!' she marvelled. 'You're going to have to give me your recipe. I might even get inspired to try it out some time.'

'Recipe is very easy,' Lin said, gesturing for Amy to move aside and let him attack the dough. 'Secret is to make sure mix is good. No pastry is good if dough is lumpy.'

Amy stood back, watching Lin work the dough with nimble fingers. Exhibiting a finesse that came from years of experience, he readied the mix, formed the loaves, and popped them in the oven in less time than it would have taken Amy to merely grease the baking pan.

'Hannibal told me you were so fast back at the prison camp that you could bake twice as many things as any other cook could in the same time, and that's how you were able to sneak extra loaves to the prisoners without drawing suspicion,' Amy said. 'At first I thought he was exaggerating, but not any more.'

'Is nothing really,' Lin said.

'Nonsense. It took a lot of courage for you to risk your life to feed American prisoners who were supposed to be your enemy.'

Lin modestly waved away the flattery and started mixing a

fresh batch of dough. 'Lin Duk Coo is not political,' he told Amy. 'Born in North Vietnam, forced to join army. They look for men who are good with guns, but I show I am better with flour and egg beater. General Kao eat some of my special bread and made me his personal chef. When he take over concentration camp, I come along and cook for everybody. I see starving prisoners and do what I must. Good cook hate to see anyone go hungry.'

'You're really something, Lin, you know that?'

Lin blushed, avoiding Amy's gaze. 'If you a friend of A-Team,' he stammered, 'if they make you a member, then *you* are really something, I think.'

'Why, thank you, Lin.'

Having prepared the latest batch of dough, Lin moved over to the far counter, where he picked up a heavy satchel. 'We have enough regular bread. Now is time to add secret ingredients.'

As Lin brought the satchel over to the other counter, Peck entered the kitchen, sniffing the air and licking his lips. 'I tell ya, Lin, I think I better start taking some of this bread down to the truck or we're going to end up eating it all up here.'

'Those loaves are probably ready to go,' Amy said, pointing to the kitchen table. 'The rest are just out of the oven, so they're still too hot to handle. How are Hannibal and Murdock coming along with the new stash. We're almost ready for them.'

'They're about finished,' Face said, loading the loaves into his arms. 'You wanna get the door for me?'

Amy held the door open while Face waddled out. Carrying seven loaves of bread was no easy task, and Peck looked like a contestant in a fraternity track meet. One got the feeling that if he completed this task without dropping any of the loaves, his next challenge would be either a sack race or trying to carry an egg in a teaspoon through fifty yards of sand. Hannibal and Murdock looked up from the coffee table where there were working and watched Face struggle towards the front hallway.

'I've got a dollar that says he won't make it.' Hannibal mumbled to Murdock.

'You're on,' Murdock said, ripping open another single serving of sugar substitute and pouring its contents into a larger plastic bag. 'Come on, Face, you can do it!' he cheered.

'I'd have a lot easier time if you'd get the door for me,' Peck grumbled, shifting his load.

'That'd be spectator interference,' Hannibal said. 'The bet would be off.'

'Sorry, Face,' Murdock apologized. 'You're on your own.'

'Thanks a lot, guys.' Reaching the front door, Peck groped awkwardly for the knob. He managed to get his fingers around it, but when he tried turning it, one of the loaves wriggled free and when Peck tried to grab it, the rest of the bread tumbled from his grasp and bounded onto the carpet. 'Oh, great. Just wonderful!'

As Peck struggled to reload his arms, Hannibal held out his hand and took a dollar from Murdock. Murdock emptied another packet into the bag, then held the bag under a hand operated sealer before adding it to the small stack of other clear sacks filled with white powder. His pet golfball was lying nearby, and Murdock picked it up for its hourly petting, lapsing into a fit of pity. 'It's easy to look the other way, isn't it, Hannibal? Injustice is always rewarded with indifference.'

'I guess,' Hannibal said, not sure what Murdock was talking about. Inspecting the loaded bags, he told his partner, 'Hey, Murdock, be sure you seal these up with no air in them.'

Murdock nodded absently, still engrossed with the plight of his globular pet. 'Like, take the injustice of the golfball-washer. There it sits, right next to the tee-off area, and all these naked little balls are put in that torture chamber, then...' Murdock pantomimed a pumping gesture as his voice quivered with emotion. 'Then they're slammed up and down, over and over and over, faster and faster, the brush bristles clawing at their little bodies...'

'Ah, still hung up on the Golfball Liberation Army, are you, Murdock?'

'That's right, Colonel. We're organized but undercapitalized.'

'Ever think about a telethon?' Hannibal suggested as he gathered up the bags and rose from the table. 'Get Arnold Palmer for a host... have Slammin' Sammy Sneed there to count the tote board and lament over all those balls he's knocked the covers off.'

As Hannibal headed for the kitchen, Murdock's eyes lit up and he exclaimed, 'Of course! That's a wonderful idea, Colonel!'

Amy emerged from the kitchen just as Hannibal was about to go in. 'Here we go, kid,' he told her, 'Ten bags of "Sweet'n'Low".'

Amy took the bags, eyeing them uncertainly. 'You think he's going to fall for this, Hannibal? I mean, he's no dummy.'

'It only has to work for a minute,' Hannibal explained. 'It's just a diversion.'

From inside the kitchen, Lin Duk Coo could be heard singing, with an accent reminiscent of John Wayne's infamous portrayal of Ghengis Khan:

'Come on boys
Lemme tell you a tale
Lemme tell you a tale
Of the ol' Chisolm Trail
Come ay-yi-yi-yi-yi
Come ay-yi-yi-yi-yi...'

'I think he's got it,' Murdock intoned. 'By Jove, He's got it!'

Hannibal matched Murdock's wretched impersonation of Henry Higgins with one of his own, declaring, 'No 'e doesn't, dear chap.'

Standing at the doorway with his reloaded arsenal of bread, Face called out, 'Hey, I hate to break up this fine revival of "My Fair Chef", but do you think somebody could leave the stage long enough to get the door for me?'

'Oh, right,' Hannibal said, coming to Peck's aid. 'Sorry about that, old boy.'

On his way out the door, Peck said, 'Remember, everybody, I need the place to myself tonight for that demonstration. I want this place spotless before you go, too.

76

Mr Toney has a reputation to live up to.'

'What kind of demonstration is it that'll take all evening, Face?' Hannibal asked, smirking suggestively.

'Hey, you know how it is with these upper crust types. They have to be wined and dined and wooed before they'll cough up any cash. Believe me, I'd rather not have to bother with it, but I've got to keep up my cover.'

'What's her name, Face?'

'Oh, you're a real card, Hannibal,' Peck cracked. 'Look, just leave the place to me for the night and go take in a show somewhere or park the van on the beach and roast marshmallows. I don't care.'

Peck left the room and staggered down the hallway, managing to reach the elevators without dropping any of the loaves. He pushed the down button with his elbow, then readjusted his load. Propping one of the loaves under his chin, he was overcome by the smell and tilted his head enough to bite off a mouthful. He savoured the flavour, chewing slowly, but when the doors opened and he stepped into one of the elevators, he almost choked. The steel wall panels were missing, revealing only the skeletal framework.

'BA!' he moaned to himself as he pushed for the garage. He counted off the floors on his way down, trying to restrain his exasperation. By the time he reached the basement, however, he was in even more of a tizzy. Stepping out of the elevator, he heard a loud noise in the adjacent car and looked to see BA dismantling the walls of that elevator as well.

'BA, what are you doing? Are you crazy?'

'Another common area bites the dust,' BA cackled with manic glee. 'Hannibal wants the truck to be armoured. This is the best stuff I could find.'

'Unbelievable,' Face muttered dismally, paying no attention to the few loaves that fell from his arms. 'Now I know how the Ancient Mariner must have felt.'

'What you talkin' about, sucker?' BA said. 'Man, step aside so I can get this panel outta here!'

As BA was manoeuvreing his way out of the elevator, two elderly women with bluish-grey hair approached from their parked car. They froze with horror at the sight of BA with his metal plating and Peck with his armload of bread.

'I'm redoing the interior of the elevators,' Peck explained lamely. 'Getting all this atrocious macho chic steel out of here. Gonna put up flocked paper... lovely pattern, believe me. We'll be finished in a day or so, Mrs Steiner. Excuse the inconvenience.'

Leaving the two women, Peck and BA toted their respective loads to the delivery truck, which was being rebuilt with certain modifications, the most notable being the addition of the elevator panels to the interior walls.

'Now all I gotta do is drill and weld these suckers into place and we'll have ourselves a tank!' BA boatsed. 'Man, we'll give that Angel dude and General Kao a bad case of the jazz!'

'That's good,' Face said, transferring bread to the racks in the back of the truck, 'because this whole affair is giving me a bad case of ulcers.'

After Peck finished loading the loaves, he brushed crumbs off his clothes and climbed out of the truck, giving BA room to work with his welding torch and electric drill. The noise emanating from inside the truck frazzled Peck's nerves even further, and he was on the verge of breaking down when he spotted a sight to take his mind off his troubles.

A taxi had pulled into the garage and come to a stop near the elevators. Gayle, Peck's dream brunette, stepped out of the back seat, carrying two loads of groceries that were almost as unwieldly in her arms as the bread had been for Peck.

'Hey, Gayle, wait! Let me give you a hand!' Peck sauntered over to her, taking the bags while she pressed for an elevator. 'What you got here?'

'Groceries,' she said. 'A couple of nice steaks, some corn on the cob, fresh squash, a pint of chocolate ice cream, a few surprises... you don't mind if I make dinner for you tonight, do you, Dr Cork?'

'No, no, not at all!' Peck said as they headed up to the first level. 'Sounds like a marvellous idea. You'll have to give me a few minutes to take care of some business up in my room.'

As the elevator doors opened and they stepped out, Gayle

said, 'Oh, absolutely. I still have to shower and slip into something . . . appropriate.'

Peck beamed with expectation as he followed Gayle through the lobby and down the hallway to her room. He was so caught up in his anticipation that he didn't notice a figure rise from the lobby sofa after they'd passed and begin following them. Angel's chauffeur, Solly, stayed a few dozen steps behind Peck and Gayle, and when he saw them stop in front of the door to condominium number nine, he ducked around the corner and waited until he heard the door open, then close. Breaking from cover, he stole down the hallway to note the number on the door, then quickly backtracked to the lobby and put a call through to his boss. Angel nodded on the third ring.

'Yeah.'

'Boss, it's Solly. I tracked 'em down.'

'You got the room they're staying in?'

'Yep. They're on the first level. Number nine.'

'Good job, Solly.'

'Thanks, boss.'

'We'll take care of 'em tonight. Hang around there until we show up.'

'You got it.'

Solly hung the phone up, pleased with himself. He wasn't aware that Peck had just left Gayle's place and headed back to the elevators for a ride up to the penthouse.

THIRTEEN

Templeton Peck prodded his fork into the last morsel of medium-rare steak and raised it to his mouth, savouring the aroma a few fleeting seconds before biting into it. 'Mmmmmmmmmmmm,' he murmured, closing his eyes. 'I don't think I've ever had such an incredible meal, Gayle.'

'I'm glad you liked it,' Gayle said, getting up from her chair and moving over to Peck, kissing him lightly on the lips. 'What do you say we retire to the living room and have some dessert before the fire?'

'Dessert?' Face groaned playfully. 'I don't think I have room for any ice cream.'

'We'll have to do something about that, won't we?' Gayle took hold of Peck's hands and helped him out of his chair. He was wearing a burgundy smoking jacket with satin trim and she was dressed in a glittering cocktail dress with a plunging neckline and a slit up one side that exposed the luxurious curve to her leg.

'Wait a second,' Peck said, breaking Gayle's grip long enough to retrieve the half-finished bottle of champagne on the table. Then, hand-in-hand, they left the kitchen and entered the living room. The whole condominium had been cleaned to Peck's specifications, and there was no sign that the other members of the A-Team had been staying there. A small cluster of logs were glowing in the hearth, throwing off their warmth through the screen. Peck set down the champagne and pointed to the sofa, telling Gayle, 'Why don't you get cozy and pour the drinks while I put some music on?'

'Going to soothe the savage beast?' Gayle teased as she sat

down.

'Only if you want me to, love.'

'I wouldn't dream of it. Play something slow and sultry.'

Peck sorted through the small collection of albums next to the stereo, but wasn't able to find anything he liked. Instead, he turned on the radio and tracked down a classical station, filling the room with the lilt of concert violins. Gayle was sprawled out on the sofa when he returned, and she shifted just enough to make room for him, then they entwined like chromosomes. After sharing a long intimate kiss, Peck came up for air and reached out with his free hand, handing Gayle her champagne, then raising his own glass for a toast. 'To a wonderful evening!'

'To a wonderful doctor!' Gayle replied.

'Uh, yeah, sure, I'll drink to that.' Peck slowly sipped his champagne, eyeing Gayle with a first glimmer of suspicion. He hadn't liked the way she'd said 'doctor'. She'd said it the way a fisherman would call out the length of trout he'd just caught that was long enough to keep. As she set her glass back down and nuzzled up close to him, though, he dismissed his paranoia and returned the embrace, letting his lips work their way up her neck and behind her ears.

'Tony,' she giggled, squirming away, 'when you kiss my earlobes, it makes me giggle.'

'I like it when you giggle,' Face whispered, continuing to nibble away.

'But when I giggle and drink champagne at the same time, I get the hiccups.'

'I like it when you hiccup, too.' Face moved in and covered her lips with his own, trying to stifle her giggling. She began to purr under the gentle persuasion of the kiss, and Peck shifted his position slightly, moving one hand down her side and around to her back, where he began to seek out the zipper that held her dress in place. Before his fingers could reach their appointed destiny, Gayle suddenly hiccuped with so much force that her whole body jerked in place, nearly ejecting Face from the sofa. As he struggled to regain his balance, Gayle hiccuped again and clasped her hand over her mouth.

'Sorry,' she apologized sheepishly. 'I warned youuuuuuu-ooooouiiiiicccccuppp!'

Neither of them could keep a straight face any further. Peck reached for the coffee table and picked up a portable console filled with push buttons. 'This should take care of you,' he said, pressing one of the buttons.

'What is that?'

'Watch!'

In response to Peck's signal, there was a whirring sound and two teak panels next to the sofa parted, revealing a portable bar. Peck took out a glass and filled it with water from a tap built into the bar, then handed it to Gayle.

'Wow!' she said.

'If the water doesn't work, I'll try something else,' Peck said. 'I'm sure there's a button for it here somewhere.'

Gayle downed the water and held her breath long enough to bring the hiccups under control, then laid back on the sofa and drew Peck close to her. 'Dr Cork to the rescue. Now, what do I owe you for your services?'

'Oh, I'm sure we can think of something.'

'You're wonderful,' Gayle whispered in Peck's ear. 'I mean it. You're not like the other professional men I've gone out with. They hardly even notice me because they're always on the phone with a client or something. But you, Tony, you've given me your undivided attention all evening. It's hard to believe I'm spending all this time with one of the top neurologists in the country.'

'Well... what can I say?' Peck said, stroking Gayle's hair. 'I just happen to be one of those guys who doesn't have trouble separating my work from my pleasure.'

'You haven't even said one thing about your job,' she remarked, taking his hand to her lips and smothering his knuckles with kisses. 'It's remarkable.'

'Ahh, it's just a job like any other job. Nerves, synapses, dendrites. Stuff like that.' Peck looked Gayle in the eyes, turning on the charm, backed by a full contingent of Mantovani strings. 'It all boils down to feeling... so, in a way, we've kinda been discussing my job all night.'

'Well, I've had enough discussion for the time being.'

Gayle put her arms around Peck and drew him close. They went with their instincts, and were about to make themselves more comfortable when the front doorbell clashed with the music pouring over the stereo.

'I don't believe it!' Peck moaned. 'I told them...'

Peck caught himself, but not in time.

'Them?' Gayle asked. 'Are you expecting some people?'

'No, that's the point.' Peck sat up and untangled himself from Gayle, then gave her another kiss. 'You stay put while I get rid of whoever it is, okay?'

'Don't be long.'

'I won't. Promise.' Peck rose to his feet and straightened his smoking jacket on his way to the door. 'I'll kill 'em!' he hissed under his breath. 'They musta had the place bugged just so they could barge in when things were getting interesting.'

'What's that, doll?' Gayle called out.

'Nothing,' Face told her. Reaching the door, he threw open the bolt and jerked the door open, prepared to see Hannibal and the others standing in the hallway. Instead, he found himself facing an elderly man in clerical garb, peering back at him over the rims of his bifocals.

'Hello, my boy.'

'Father O'Malley!?' Face couldn't believe his eyes. 'What are you doing here. When I came to visit you at the orphanage last month, you were in bad shape and confined to your bed!'

'The Lord looks after His own,' the priest said. 'I've made a splendid recovery, if I must say so myself. But that's not why I've come. Sorry to call on you unannounced, my boy, but something's come up and I thought it was important enough to merit a visit.'

Father O'Malley was one of two priests, the other being the ailing Monsignor Magill, who ran the St Bartholomew Orphanage, where Templeton Peck had been raised from infancy up to the time of his enlistment in the Armed Forces. The two men were the closest Peck had come to having a true father, and he could hardly send O'Malley off after the priest had travelled miles to visit him.

'Come on in, Father,' Peck offered.

'Am I interrupting anything?' O'Malley inquired, peering inside the apartment. A wall prevented him from having a view of the living room.

'Of course not,' Face chuckled nervously. 'Just watching a little TV, playing some canasta. You now, regular Saturday night stuff.'

From the living room, Gayle cried out playfully, Tooony, I miiiiiiss youuuuuuu!!!'

Peck's cheeks changed colour and he glanced away from Father O'Malley, who remained out in the hallway. 'I'll make this as fast as I can, lad.' He reached into the folds of his robes and withdrew a small jewellery box, which he handed to Face. 'Yesterday at the orphanage I received a package marked "urgent". Inside was this box, along with a letter asking me to please get it to you. It was signed by a Leslie Becktall.'

The surprise Peck had felt at seeing Father O'Malley in the hallway was minute compared to the jolt that ran through him when he heard Leslie's name and opened the jewellery box to find a fraternity pin. It was as if he'd pried open a long-sealed Pandora's box filled with old memories. He stood in a daze, staring at the pin.

'Do you know Leslie Becktall?' Father O'Malley asked. 'Templeton, lad, are you all right?'

Peck nodded feebly. He noticed a note folded into the lid of the jewellery box and quickly took it out. As he read the hand-written message, his eyes widened and his heartbeat quickened. 'Father,' he gasped, 'where did this come from?'

'The postmark was Cayambe, Ecuador,' the Reverend replied, removing a scrap of worn paper from another pocket. 'I still have the original envelope if you'd care to see it.'

'Yes, yes.'

O'Malley watched Peck as the younger man scanned the envelope for more clues. 'I trust this was good news for you, then?'

'I'm not sure yet,' Peck confessed, 'but you've sure got my heart beating. Thanks for coming by, Father. Thanks a hell

84

of a ... oops, sorry.'

'That's quite all right, lad. I've heard the word often.'

'Well, listen, would you like to have something to drink or a snack or something?' Peck asked. 'I have –'

'Tooooooony,' Gayle beckoned once more from the living room. 'Hurry up, doctor, I want to be examined . . .'

'In a second!' Face retorted impatiently.

Father O'Malley placed a hand on Peck's shoulder and winked. 'I think I'd better let you get back to your canasta. I was planning to stop down the street and visit Father Charles before heading back to the orphanage, anyway. It was good to see you, Templeton.'

'Goodnight, Father,' Peck said, giving O'Malley a light hug. 'And really, thanks so much.'

'Any time, my boy, any time.' Before turning to leave, O'Malley looked Peck over a final time and smiled. 'I love your jacket. It looks like something Don Ameche would wear when wooing his sweethearts in the movies. You're in good company.'

'Thanks again, Father.'

Peck closed the door and remained in the hallway a moment, re-reading the note and staring again at the fraternity pin. A strong feeling of resolve came over him, and he closed the box and slipped it into the pocket of his smoking jacket as he hurried back into the living room.

'Who was that?' Gayle asked, slithering across the sofa and grabbing Face as he walked by, trying to find the boa she'd worn up to the penthouse. 'I got lonesome waiting for you.'

'One of the kids from the orphanage where I grew up fell off a slide and broke his leg,' Peck adlibbed, grabbing the boa off the end table. 'I have to get him into surgery right away.'

As Peck hoisted Gayle from the sofa and guided her to the front door, she wondered, 'Why do they need a neurologist for that?'

'You have no idea how many nerves end up in the leg,' Peck said, throwing the boa over Gayle's shoulders. Pausing before the door, he gave her a quick kiss and told her, 'I hate to smooch and run, but I hope you'll understand.'

Peck opened the door, but Gayle wasn't ready to leave. 'Why don't I just wait here for you to come back?' she volunteered. 'I could rub your tired back when you get out of surgery.'

'No, I'm always in a terrible mood after surgery,' Face countered, easing Gayle out the door. 'Look, I'll call you next time I have some free time. Thanks for a wonderful evening, Gayle.'

'Sure, Tony. Sure.' Gayle eyed him uncertainly, then headed down the hallway.

Once he was alone inside the penthouse, Peck pulled out the jewellery box and pried the lid open again. Staring at the pin, he whispered nostaligically, 'Leslie...'

FOURTEEN

They were at a college party. Peck was in his senior year, a veritable Big Man on campus. Fraternity president, track team captain, member of the Dean's list – the whole works. As usual, he was being the life of the party, playing the field, fending off advances from half a dozen girls, all the while keeping his eyes on a certain young woman who'd come to the party late and had retreated to a corner, where she shyly kept to herself, picking up magazines or stray newspapers to give her a diversion from the discomfort she was feeling. She would occasionally look up and out at the party, her eyes filled with a strange mixture of hunger and aloofness, as if she wanted to be a part of the festivities and yet somehow couldn't bring herself to put on a false front of frivolous gaiety. Several times Peck caught her eye and offered an inviting smile, and in each instance she returned the slightest upturning of her lips before looking away. As the night dragged on, Peck became more and more intrigued with her, and finally broke away from his throng of friends to seek her out, only to find that she'd just left. Cursing himself for having put off his desire to meet her, he dashed out the door, staring wildly into the night in the hope of finding her. There was a light mist in the air, forming halos around streetlights and making the ground glisten and tyres hiss as cars sped down the road past dormitory row. He'd asked someone her name before leaving, and as he paced down the sidewalk looking for her, he called her name out loud, 'Leslie. Leslie.' And then at last he spotted her, walking across the quad, her hair flowing about her head in the stiff breeze that had suddenly picked up, He called her name again and began to run after her. She took a few more steps, then stopped and looked back at him, wiping a strand of hair from her face.

'Leslie, wait.' He felt foolish and giddy in a way he'd never felt before. He was certain that he had just begun a part of his life that would be filled with an enviable magic, that in the person of this young woman who stood waiting for him he might find the key to a special sort of happiness that had eluded him during all his years at the orphanage.

'Leslie,' he called out again, his voice filled with passion.

'Sorry, Face. It's just me.'

Peck jerked himself from his sleep and saw Hannibal leaning over him, holding the jewellery box with the fraternity pin. Peck realized he'd fallen asleep on the sofa.

'Hannibal?' he mumbled sleepily.

'That's right, Face,' Hannibal told him. 'Welcome to the real world. That must have been some dream you were having. You had a grin that woulda put the Cheshire Cat to shame. We've been here almost half an hour, but we didn't have the heart to wake you.'

BA and Murdock were also in the living room. Murdock was fiddling with the remote console, making TV screens drop out of the ceiling, turning on the kitchen toaster oven, activating the air conditioner and otherwise wreaking low-level havoc throughout the condo.

'Hey, be careful with that, Murdock, would you?' Face pleaded. 'It's a miracle you haven't broken anything yet. Don't mess up a good thing.'

BA crossed his arms as he plopped into the chair closest to the fireplace. 'I sure hope you had a good time last night, sucker,' he told Peck. 'We had to crash in the van and I got cricks in my neck.'

'You guys are never going to believe what happened!' Peck blurted out, then proceeded to relate the events of the previous evening, concentrating primarily on the visit from Father O'Malley and the strange parcel he'd brought. Hannibal nodded agreeably throughout the discourse, but when Peck began laying out a proposed plan of action based on the message he'd received along with the fraternity pin, his head stopped moving and his expression changed drastically.

'You're right,' he finally interrupted. 'I don't believe what you're saying, Face. You want us to go to Equador to hunt up the "Sweetheart of Sigma Chi"?'

'Exactly!' Peck said excitedly. 'We have to, and the sooner the better!'

Hannibal tossed the jewellery box over to BA, then shook his head at Peck. 'I think all this high living has finally made your brain go soft, my friend. Even if we weren't in the middle of an assignment, I'd still have to say this has to be one of the goofiest nutbar proposals I've heard since we started up the team, and if it came from anybody else I'd already be showing them the door.'

'Look, we'll be done with Angel and General Kao by this afternoon, provided all goes well,' Peck said. 'After that, our schedule's free, right? Right?'

Hannibal didn't reply. As Murdock continued toying with the remote, BA examined the contents of the jewellery box and made a sour face. 'Is this all she sent back? One cheap cufflink? Man, you gotta be hard up to get excited –'

'It's my fraternity pin and it isn't cheap, BA,' Face said. Appealing to the others, he went on, 'Look, you guys, we've gone on cases for each other before. I don't see why we can't go on one for me.'

'For one thing,' Hannibal began, 'we don't even know this girl's in any trouble. She stood you up in college fifteen years ago and finally decided to write. I'd say you were better off without her.'

'I know Leslie,' Peck insisted. 'I can tell by the tone in her letter that something's wrong.'

'Which part tips you off?' Hannibal asked. 'The part about "no words can express the sorrow I've felt all these years", or "you'll always have a special place in my soul"?'

'What about this?' Peck took the letter out of his shirt pocket and unfolded it, then read, '"In everyone's life, there comes a time when it's necessary to call up the past and face it. In my life the time is now."'

BA set the frat pin down on the coffee table and complained, 'Man, that sounds like somethin' out of one of them goofy greetings cards with two fools walkin' down some beach.'

'I'm telling you, I *know* Leslie and she'd never write something like that unless there was something wrong!' Peck maintained.

Before anyone could respond, Murdock triggered a button that brought a queen-sized bed rolling out from the wall, covered with satin sheets.

'Nice touch,' Hannibal cracked.

BA asked Peck, 'What's she doing in Ecuador anyhow?'

'I have no idea!' Face cried out, overcome with frustration. He got up from the sofa and began pacing. I'm telling you, I never heard another word about Leslie Becktall since the day she stood me up for a date halfway through my last semester in school. It's like she dropped out of existence.'

'Tough break,' Hannibal said. 'Shook you up, did it?'

'I quit school and joined the Marines right afterwards,' Peck said. 'That's all ... Listen, are you guys going to help me or not?'

'We'll think about it, Face,' Hannibal said. Right now, though, we've got our work cut out for us. The truck's all ready, but there's still a few other –'

Hannibal stopped in mid-sentence as the front door suddenly swung open. Amy and Lin Duck Coo rushed in, both of them breathless from exertion.

'What's with you two?' BA asked them. 'You look like you just got back from a track meet!'

'Downstairs ...' Amy gasped, 'Some kind of trouble ... guys with guns shot up one of the rooms.'

'What? When?' Hannibal asked, immediately on his guard.

Amy paused to catch her breath, then explained. Just before Lin and I got back from the newspaper. There was a big crowd gathered in the lobby, and someone said that two men with machine guns had just riddled one of the condos down the hall. Fortunately, there was no one home at the time, but, still, it seems too much –

'Oh, no!' Face shouted, cutting Amy short. 'What was the number of the place that got hit.'

'I don't really remember...'

'Nine,' Peck said. 'Was it number nine?'

'Yes!' Lin exclaimed. 'They say number nine!'

'Gayle! That's where Gayle was staying!' Peck said excitedly.

'Gayle?'

'The woman I was with last night. She was staying in number nine with a friend. I was just there yesterday, helping her take groceries in and... oh oh...'

'Are you thinking what I'm thinking?' Hannibal asked Peck. Without waiting for an answer, Hannibal looked back at Amy and Lin. 'Do either of you remember if anyone followed you up here?'

'I don't know,' Amy said. I don't think so, but we weren't checking...'

'Those guns were meant for us,' Hannibal said, rushing over to the cedar chest in the far corner of the living room. Raising the lid, he started pulling out weapons and passing them around. 'Something tells me we aren't going to make it to Indian Dunes this morning.'

As pistols and rifles changed hands, the group heard a rumbling outside the building. It grew louder by the second, and finally they could see a helicopter hovering in position less than twenty-five feet from the main picture-window. Solly was riding on the passenger's side, and he swung open the chopper door to point a submachine gun at the window.

'Hit the deck!' Hannibal shouted, diving down onto the carpet. The others followed suit, just as the plate glass window shattered under the bevy of bullets that pounded into the living room, devastating the decor.

Lin Duk Coo was closest to the window, hiding behind a marble pedestal that had supported an antique vase that was now little more than a collection of scattered fragments. The chef peered out from his cover, managing to get a good look at the helicopter. 'General Kao in chopper! he shouted.

Inside the 'copter, the general had spotted Lin at the same time, and he pointed over Solly's shoulder in the direction of the pedestal. 'Kill him!' he ordered. 'I want Lin Duk Coo dead!'

The pilot guided the aircraft closer to the building, and Solly sent another shower of bullets pouring into the condominium. Lin Duk Coo reeled away from the pedestal and crawled along the carpet to the safety of the kitchen. At the same time, Peck wriggled his way to the bedroom and peered out through the window there. 'They're on the right, Hannibal!' he shouted over his shoulder, quickly retreating from the room as the helicopter paused outside the window and Solly shattered the glass with yet another burst of gunfire.

By now the others had backed into the front entryway. No one had been seriously injured, although Lin and BA both bled from superficial cuts caused by flying glass. They waited, listening to the helicopter pass by every window of the condominium so that Solly could fire into the building. Finally, the din of crashing glass and gunshots subsided and the drone of rotors faded slightly.

'Sounds like they're landing on the roof,' Hannibal said. 'We better make our move before we get trapped in here. Murdock, the chopper's your assignment. Lin and Amy, you're with Murdock.'

'Right, Colonel,' Murdock said.

'Are you okay, Lin?' Hannibal asked.

Lin wiped away the blood on his cheek and forearm, claiming, 'These are just scratches. It take more than cuts to stop Lin Duk Coo.'

'Okay,' Hannibal said. 'Face, BA, let's get to the truck and just hope we don't run into too large a welcome-wagon on the way . . . '

FIFTEEN

Word of the gunplay on the first level had already spread throughout the entire building by the time General Kao's helicopter had begun circling the upper floors, allowing Solly to vent windows with bursts of machine gun fire. A general panic had overcome the tower, and when Hannibal led BA and Peck out of the penthouse, they found the hallway crowded with frantic tenants who looked like sinners caught unprepared by the Day of Judgement.

'It's terrorists!' someone shrieked. 'And the Olympics haven't even started yet!'

Stella, the voluptuous redhead who had got Mr Yerkovitch on to the A-Team for cluttering a common area with auto parts, now looked upon that same group of undesirables as if they were a cross between a three-man US Cavalry and St George's Royal Order of Dragon Slayers. 'Mr Toney, Mr Toney!' she whined, falling on him like a supplicant. 'What's going on? you have to help us!'

As he waded through the crowd, Peck shook Stella loose and shouted, loud enough for all to hear, 'Everybody get in your apartments! Lock the doors and stay low. They aren't after you!'

Mob psychology being what it is, the tenants were wary of separating, feeling a vague sense of safety in numbers. They continued to mingle around Hannibal, Peck, and BA as the three men tried to reach the elevators. Outside the tower, Solly spewed more rounds into the penthouse, shattering more glass. Several errant bullets found their way through the front doorway, just missing Dr Peters, who promptly fainted, causing his wife to go into hysterics, thinking he'd

93

been shot.

'You heard the man!' Hannibal echoed. 'Get to your rooms and stay there!'

'Now!' BA roared for emphasis, sending the tenants scattering. Not all of them dwelled on the top floor, though, and several people accompanied the A-Team to the elevators, including Stella. The lit numbers over the elevators indicated that one was on the first floor and the other was down in the basement garage.

'We can't wait that long,' Hannibal said. 'Face, where's the stairs?'

'Over here,' someone answered before Face could. The voice was familiar, and when the men looked where it had come from, they saw Don standing in the stairwell doorway, along with two other men brandishing Uzi submachine guns. There were a handful of people between them and the A-Team, and Don reached out, grabbing Stella before Peck or the others could raise their weapons.

'Let her go,' Hannibal told Don.

Don shook his head. 'Drop your guns or she dies,' he warned. To the other residents, he shouted, 'Everyone else get outta here or you'll all look like switchboards!'

As the tenants dispersed with frightened haste, Stella squirmed futilely in Don's grasp. Hannibal hesitated a moment, then leaned over and set his gun down on the carpet. Peck and BA followed suit.

'Here's one time we coulda used that fool Murdock guardin' our rear,' BA grumbled under his breath.

'Yeah,' Face agreed glumly. 'Sorry, guys, I guess –'

'Shut up!' Don bellowed, waiting until his cohorts had retrieved the fallen weapons before shoving Stella away from him. The woman staggered on her high-heels, hyperventilating her way around the corner. When one of the elevators opened, Don gestured for the prisoners to get in. 'Move it! The boss'll want a few words with you before we take care of you for good.'

'Oh, goody,' Hannibal drawled, stepping into the elevator. 'I just love a stay of execution. You gonna give us a last meal, too? I'm starved.'

94

'Only if you like eating lead,' Don told him. As the doors closed on the six men, Don pulled a walkie-talkie from his back pocket and spoke into it. 'We got three of 'em. Set 'er down and mop up!'

Out in the helicopter, Solly replied, 'Gotcha!' The pilot had overheard Don's transmission, and he guided the chopper to a landing atop the flattest section of the tower roof. Solly reloaded his machine gun, then started out, telling General Kao, 'Stay up here, sir. We got three of 'em. I'll be back with the rest.'

'I want Lin!' General Kao snapped from the back seat of the helicopter. 'If you can, bring him to me alive so that I can be the one to see to my own revenge.'

'I'll see what I can do,' Solly said, stepping down to the roof and shouting above the roar of rotors, 'I can't make any promises, though.'

'Dead or alive, I want him!'

Solly snapped off a mock salute, then crouched over and ran clear of the sweeping overhead blade to the stairwell entrance. Bounding hurriedly down the steps, he burst into the penthouse corridor, waving his gun before him like an evil magician's magic wand. The only people in the hallway were the Peters couple. Dr Peters was just coming to, thanks to the attention of his wife. As Solly headed towards them, though, it was Mrs Peters who swooned, sprawling across her husband. The gunman wasn't interested in them, however. Striding past them, he paused a moment outside the bullet-riddled door to Mr Toney's penthouse, then kicked it open and charged inside, ready for anything.

The entire suite looked like a warzone. Solly waded through the rubble towards the main bathroom, where he heard a shower being turned off.

'All right!' he called out, 'Get out here, real slow like!'

A few seconds passed, then Amy pulled open the bathroom door and stepped into the open, wearing one towel around her torso and another around her hair. Seeing the gunman and the rubble around him, she gasped, 'What's going on here? I . . . I was just in the shower, not more than

95

ten minutes, and look what happens?!!'

'Who do you think you're kidding, lady?'

'You, Amy smirked. She'd provided enough of a diversion to get Solly to turn his back to the entryway closet, and Lin Duk Coo suddenly burst out from cover at him.

'Ay-yi-yi!' the chef howled.

As Solly swung around to meet his attacker, Murdock popped up from behind the sofa and made a quick overarm throw with his golfball, catching Solly in the back of the head.

'Fore!' Murdock yelled as Solly slumped to the carpet. Lin jumped on top of the gunman, wresting away his weapon. Solly wasn't offering much resistance, though. He was out cold.

'Good job, Murdock,' Amy said, unwrapping the towel around her to reveal that she was wearing shorts and a tube-top.

'So much for this guy,' Murdock said, taking the machine gun from Lin. 'Now let's get that bird on the roof...'

SIXTEEN

Tom Angel was swearing loudly as he tried to jam a key into the side door of the bakery truck when Don led his prisoners out of the basement.

'We got the locks changed, Lieutenant,' Hannibal said with a grin. 'You know us, always trying to be difficult.'

The other two gunmen kept BA and Peck under guard as Don gave Hannibal a shove in the direction of the truck. Angel yanked a revolver out of his coat pocket and aimed it at Hannibal, ordering, 'Open it or I waste you right here.'

'Say please,' Hannibal joked, keeping his hands above his head as Don frisked him and came up with a set of keys.

'Going to be a comedian all the way to the grave, is that it, Colonel?' Angel said.

'A grave? I'm flattered, Lieutenant.' Hannibal took the keys and sorted out the one that worked the truck door. 'I didn't think you'd bother with accommodation for me. I had this foolish idea you'd just dump my body off to the side of some country road so I could ruin some poor jogger's day.'

Once Hannibal had opened the door, Don pulled him aside and Angel inspected the interior. Noticing the reinforced walls and other modifications, he said, 'What the hell did you do to this thing?'

'Oh, we just figured that if you were going to be transporting drugs, you'd want something a little sturdier than a mere truck,' Peck ventured from the background. 'It took us a lot of work, but because we're such nice guys, we won't charge you for it.'

'Well, let's see how much you tampered with the bread.' Angel took one of Lin's replacement loaves and broke it open in the middle, exposing a plastic bag filled with whit[e] powder. After dabbing his fingertip into the mixture, Ang[el] tasted it, then threw the loaf down with disgust. 'Who th[e] hell do you think you're trying to kid, Colonel?'

'There must be some kind of mistake,' Hannibal sai[d] reaching for another of the loaves. 'Here, I think this is th[e] one we're looking for.'

The loaf was the largest of the entire batch, and for goo[d] reason. Baked inside it was a sawn-off shotgun, and whe[n] Hannibal poked his fingers through the crust and found th[e] trigger, he demonstrated that the weapon worked just fin[e]. His first shot blew away the barrel of Don's Uzi, and th[e] second sent the other two gunmen diving for cover. Befor[e] Angel could overcome his surprise and get off a shot with h[is] revolver, Hannibal bowled him to the ground and darte[d] inside the delivery truck, pulling the doors closed behin[d] him. BA and Peck, who had foreseen the disruption, brok[e] for the nearest group of parked cars and quickly conceale[d] themselves from the view of their captors.

'You won't get away from me!' Angel vowed, crawlin[g] across the pavement after his gun, which had clattered awa[y] from him. Before he could reach it, though, Hannibal ha[d] the truck started up in gear. Angel had to dive to one side t[o] avoid being run over by the same tyres that crushed his gu[n]. Don's cohorts pumped their Uzis for all they were worth, b[ut] the reinforced plating kept the bullets from causing anythin[g] more than cosmetic damage to the truck.

Spotting Peck and BA to his left, Hannibal jerked hard o[n] the steering wheel and applied the brakes, spinning the truc[k] around in a half-circle so that they could slip in through th[e] side door without exposing themselves to the submachin[e] guns of Angel's men.

'Nice goin', Hanibal!' BA said.

'Half the thanks goes to Lin,' Hannibal said. 'He's the on[ly] guy I know who could bake a loaded gun inside a loaf [of] bread without blowing up the oven.'

As it turned out, Lin had doctored more than just one loa[f]. BA ripped into a baguette to get at a pair of .22s, and Pec[k] liberated an Uzi of his own from a large loaf of sourdoug[h]

98

While Hannibal completed his circle with the truck, BA shifted the elevator walls across the opening in the side doors, revealing two gun ports he'd welded that allowed both he and Peck to fire at the enemy without exposing more than a couple of square inches of target area.

It didn't take long for Angel's men to realize the futility of wasting more ammo on the truck. They fled from the gunfire and scrambled into their limousine, which had been parked at an angle, taking up three parking spaces. Fortunately for them, the vehicle had been backed in, and they were able to race from the parking structure before Hannibal could jockey the truck completely around to give chase.

'Damn!' BA cursed. 'We almost had 'em!'

'Look on the bright side,' Peck told him, 'They almost had us, too!'

'They aren't out of this yet, anyway,' Hannibal reminded them as he finally got the truck faced the right way. 'Remember, we've still got our rear guard!'

'Come on, Murdock!' Peck muttered. 'Don't let us down!'

Even as Peck was speaking, Murdock was holding a quick conference with Amy and Lin Duk Coo at the top of the stairwell leading to the roof.

'Here, Lin,' Murdock said, handing Solly's machine gun to the chef. 'When Amy opens the door, you fire out and keep me covered. Make sure you aim to my right.'

'What are you going to do?' Amy asked Murdock.

Murdock sucked in his gut and tilted his cap to one side before declaring, 'The Range Rider's gonna try to rassle himself a chopper, on a count of three. One...'

Amy moved to the door and clasped her hand around the knob, Lin took a deep breath and cradled the machine gun in his arms.

'Two...'

Amy turned the doorknob as far as she could but kept the door shut. Lin rested his right index finger against the trigger and pointed the gun at the door.

'Three!'

The door flew open and Murdock bolted out, leaning

slightly to the left so that the stream of gunfire to his right stayed clear of him. As he hoped, the element of surprise and the spray of bullets created a few needed seconds of confusion aboard the helicopter. General Kao leapt behind the pilots seat for protection, clinging to the pilot's arm and preventing him from reaching his instruments. By the time the pilot had shaken the General loose and manned the controls for lift-off, Murdock was on the skids and opening the door to the driver's seat. When the pilot reached out to shove Murdock away, Murdock locked his fingers around the other man's wrist and held tight as he jumped from the skid. Gravity did the rest. As Murdock dropped back to the roof, he took the pilot with him. However, the pilot was jerked at such an angle that he didn't clear the doorway and instead banged his head hard against the shell of the chopper with enough force to knock himself out. In the meantime, Amy and Lin had run around to the other side, apprehending General Kao as he tried to disembark from the helicopter.

'We meet again, General,' Lin leered, pointing the machine gun at Kao. 'Maybe now I am wanting revenge as bad as you.'

The general stopped and eyed the gun, trying not to show fear. 'You will not shoot me.'

'That is what you say,' Lin retorted coldly.

'Lin, don't!' Amy intervened. 'Let the authorities take care of him.'

'He deserves to die!' Lin spat.

'That's not for you to decide, Lin!' Amy grabbed a length of cable from inside the helicopter and moved behind Kao to bind his wrists together. 'Go help Murdock get the pilot out of the cockpit!'

By the time Amy had finished tying the knots that bound General Kao to the frame of a large television antenna, Murdock and Lin had similarly secured the unconscious pilot to an air-conditioning unit.

'Okay, let's get outta here and see how the rest of the gang's doin'!' Murdock said, breaking for the helicopter.

'Do you know how to fly one of these?' Amy asked as she

followed him.

'Hey, you fly one, you fly 'em all,' Murdock boasted. Once he'd climbed into the driver's seat, however, he noticed that the instrument console readings were all in Chinese. 'Well, maybe it'll be a little tricky, after all...'

Amy took the passenger's seat, then stared out of the window at Lin, who was standing before General Kao. She shouted, 'Come on, Lin!'

Lin lingered a moment longer, glaring at Kao. 'Miss Allen is right. Is best you stand trial, so everyone can learn that General Kao is lowest of low. I will be in courtroom, laughing inside at you. The revenge is mine for all those you tortured!'

General Kao said nothing. He stared down at his feet as Lin rushed over and climbed aboard the helicopter and plopped into the back seat.

'Hang onto your hats, boys and girls, ' Murdock said, clamping his fingers around a lever and throttle. 'Here goes nothin...'

Murdock's intuition served him well, as he managed to lift the chopper from the roof and out into the open air.

'Ay-yi-yi-yi!' Lin howled triumphantly. 'Up, up, and awayyyyyyy!'

'Yes indeedy!' Murdock said, gaining confidence with each testing of the controls. 'Look out, world! Here comes the Golfball Liberation Army!'

Executing a perfect trim-and-bank manoeuvre, Murdock shifted the chopper's course and descended swiftly towards the lower floors of the building, just as Tom Angel's limousine was shooting up the ramp leading from the underground garage to the streets. The bakery truck was more than fifty yards behind and losing ground every second to the swifter limo.

'Smokes out and seat belts on, gang!' Murdock announced. 'We're in for a rough ride!'

Gunning the throttle, Murdock dipped the chopper sharply to one side, just managing to drop in front of the limousine as it was about to clear the parking lot. Behind the wheel, Angel was forced to swerve to one side and change course drastically in the hope of reaching the back exit from the lot. By then, however, the delivery truck was back in the thick of the chase, and a few well-placed shots from Peck and BA blew out the limo's front tyres. Angel tried driving on the rims, but it was a lost cause. The truck caught up with them on one side while the helicopter kept hovering nearby on the other. After BA shot out several of the limo windows, Angel's men had had enough. They tossed their guns out the window and waved their arms in gestures of surrender. Left with no avenue of escape, Angel was forced to stop the limousine and pound his fist on the dashboard with frustration.

'Damn it, I was so close!' he fumed. 'So damn close!'

As Murdock landed the helicopter nearby, Hannibal got out of the delivery truck and strolled over to the limousine, followed by BA and Peck.

'It's just not your day, Tommy,' Hannibal said as the A-Team escorted Angel and his men out of the limo and into the back of the bakery truck. 'This is the end of the line. The dope's in there with you. See if you can find it before the police arrive. Maybe between the bunch of you you can eat enough of the evidence to beat the rap... of course, I wouldn't want to be in your shoes with that much poison rattling around in my system. This is a long way from Haight Ashbury.'

Surrounded by his broken men in the back of the truck, Angel looked less like a crime kingpin than an overgrown schoolboy who'd been caught playing one too many pranks during lunch break. He made a petulant face at Hannibal and vowed, 'My father will have you killed.'

Hannibal shook his head as he helped himself to his first cigar of the day. After blowing smoke in Angel's face, he advised him, 'You tell your father if I get angry enough, I might just come to Phoenix and wash him out, too. Tell him to keep his head down, because I could be the postman or the guy who cleans his pool. Who knows, I might even be his caddy.'

Hannibal slammed the rear doors shut and locked them. Hearing one of the men inside grab for the door handle, BA shouted, 'Hey, fool, when we changed the locks we made it so you can't get out from inside. You're wastin' your time!'

'Now, now, BA., don't rub it in ,' Hannibal told Baracus. 'Why don't you go get the van so we can get outta here? I hate crowds.'

It seemed that half the residents of both towers had converged on the parking lot to witness the apprehension of Angel and his men. Dr Peters was among them, and he stepped forward, addressing Peck.

'I say, Mr Toney, there must be some explanation for all this. What's going on? Who are these people?'

Dr Peters was looking at the rest of the A-Team, who were waiting for BA to show up with the van. Amy stepped forward to explain. 'We're Mr Toney's friends. The guys in the truck are obviously not. There's two more on the roof, both Vietnamese nationals. One of them's a war criminal named Kao. A third man is probably still out cold in Mr Toney's model apartment.'

BA pulled up in the van and the A-Team climbed in while Peck told Peters, 'Apologize to Mr Yerkovitch for the damages. I'll try and make it good. By the way, the walls of the elevators are in that bakery truck ... and I guess Sunday brunch is off.'

'But,but –'

'Give my love to everyone,' Peck said. Joining his associates in the van, he looked to the crowd gathered round and blew them all a kiss, shouting out the window as BA drove off, 'Ciao ...!'

SEVENTEEN

With Mr Toney's penthouse suite rendered uninhabitable, the A-Team was forced to relocate its operational head-quarters. The nod went to BA's rundown apartment on the other side of town, far from the media focus that was expected to centre around the day's commotion at Century Towers. A generous appraisal of BA's sense for interior design might have included adjectives such as 'rustic' or 'homely'. Hannibal was more to the point.

'A real funkhole you got here, BA,' he said, taking in the cluttered surroundings.

'Yeah, pretty cozy, ain't it?' BA said proudly, removing an orange crate filled with records from one of the padded chairs so he could sit down. 'Place where a man can feel at home.'

'Yeah?' Peck taunted, 'Then maybe next time we'll come here first instead of ruining one of my gigs. I hope you guys realize two of my best scams went down the toilet on account of me being such a "team player". You owe me, and I know just how you're gonna pay up.'

'Not that Equador trip again,' Hannibal groaned. 'I was kinda hoping you'd have forgotten about it in all the excitement.'

'No way,' Face insisted.

Amy was on the phone in the corner, and she interrupted the team's bickering by picking up her end of the conversation with the person she'd called. 'Okay. Okay. That's great. I'll bring Lin down to the paper this afternoon. Right. Right. Thanks. Yeah, well that's what being a reporter is all about, you know ... hitting the big ones. Uh huh, okay, bye.'

Hanging up the phone, Amy turned brightly to face the others.

'Everything work out?' Murdock called out from the floor, where he was playing with his pet golfball, rolling it back and forth across the carpet.

When Amy nodded, Peck crossed his arms and sulked, 'I'm glad at least somebody is coming out on the good end of all this.'

Peck swung his feet up on the coffee table. BA glared at him and shouted, 'Git your feet offa my table, man. You're leavin' scuff marks on the finish!'

Peck dropped his feet and looked at the scarred and faded surface of the tabletop. 'How can you tell?'

'Don't give me none of that highbrow jive, Face!'

'My, aren't we touchy!'

Hannibal turned to Amy and asked, 'So Lin's all set?'

'Yep,' Amy replied. 'They're going to send some people from the US Embassy down to the paper this afternoon to work out arrangements for diplomatic immunity. Lin'll be able to stay in the States.'

'Hey, that's great!' BA said.

Murdock traded smiles with his golfball, then rose to his feet and carried the ball over to where Amy was jotting down a few notes from her phone call.

'You know, Amy, you're a big-time reporter now...' he stammered, fumbling for the right words. 'I mean, a Vietnamese war criminal and an underworld kingpin's son busted for trafficking in heroin... I was wondering... maybe you could, like, do a story on what's happening to golfballs. We need some heat, Amy. Something to focus the world on our plight.' Trying to find more ammunition for his cause, he added, almost as an afterthought, 'The Golfball Liberation Army is a non-violent group...'

Amy looked past Murdock and rolled her eyes as she tried to keep a straight face. 'Maybe a human interest bit chronicling life in the cellophane package?' she suggested with thinly veiled sarcasm. 'A series maybe?'

'Wouldja?' Murdock yipped excitedly. 'Wouldja?'

Amy smirked and reached out for his golfball. As she put it in her purse, she told Murdock, 'Anything for a good cause.'

'All right!' Murdock pulled off his hat and waved it in the air as he hopped up and down. 'The movement begins!'

'Man, you need some movement back to the hospital!' BA complained. 'You need to be shrink-wrapped, Murdock!'

Before the ongoing rift between BA and Murdock could escalate, Lin entered the living room from the kitchen, carrying a small tray. He eyed the group expectantly. 'Lin have good news?'

'That's right,' Hannibal told him. 'You're gonna get to stay in this country. Amy's paper arranged it. You're gonna get a chance to be a US citizen.'

Lin's eyes misted and he stood in place for several seconds, filled with emotion. As if to change the subject, he held the tray out, revealing his latest baked concoction. His voice cracked as he explained, 'I made fortune cookies... an old recipe. Not like store-bought.' Setting the tray on the coffee table, he added, 'A-Team is my best friend, I think... you saved my life.'

'One good turn deserves another, Lin,' Hannibal told the chef. 'If you hadn't slipped us food back in that prison camp, we wouldn't be here right now. And, speaking of right now, maybe you better scoot home and change into something besides that chef's outfit you've been wearing the past few days. You want to make a good impression with the folks from the embassy.'

Lin nodded and wiped away his tears with the back of his hand, then quickly went around, shaking hands with the men of the A-Team. 'We see plenty of each other now, okay?' he asked the group.

'You bet,' Hannibal said.

Amy told Lin, 'There's a few of your things out in the van. I'll go out with you to get them and show you where the bus-stop is.'

Lin shook his head. 'I'll just get my things. I want to walk home and enjoy how it feels to at last be a free man!'

Amy and Lin waved a final farewell to the men, then left

106

the apartment. Hannibal was the first one to grab for a fortune cookie and break it open. A fortune fell out onto his lap.

'What's it say, Hannibal?' Murdock asked.

Hannibal picked up the slip of paper and read the message to himself, then laughed lightly. 'It says, "I love it when a plan comes together"'

'Nice touch, Lin,' BA mumbled, reaching for another cookie.

'While we're on the subject of plans,' Peck said, 'I insist that we get down to Equador and look into what's happening with Leslie.'

'Oh, Face, please,' Hannibal said. 'Look, didn't she leave a phone number or something? Maybe you could send a telegram . . .'

Face stood up and started pacing around the coffee table, haranguing his associates. 'You guys are really something, you know that? After all the stuff I do for this team you don't think I'm important enough or my case is good enough? Is that it?'

'Hey, we just finished a job, man!' BA said. 'We ain't even had a chance to rest yet!'

Amy returned just as Peck was clapping his hands together, having arrived at a decision. 'Okay, if that's the way you guys are going to be about it, I only have one other way to go. I'm hiring the A-Team!'

'I hate to ask this question,' Amy said, eyeing Peck strangely, 'but what's going on?'

Peck ignored Amy and stared at Hannibal, BA and Murdock. 'Well, what do you say? I'm tellin' you, you guys owe me!'

'Face, this is crazy!' Hannibal said. 'We'd be stealing your money on a wild goose chase. Look, maybe –'

'Is it a deal?' Peck pressed. 'I want an answer. Yes or no!'

Hannibal looked at BA and Murdock, then shrugged his shoulders. 'It's a deal. But since you're the client, someone else monitors the cash for this case.'

'You think I'm gonna stiff you?' Face asked, incredulous.

'Face, it's a conflict of interest. We don't wanna get paid in

IOUs.' Hannibal looked at Amy. 'We'll let her manage the money on this one.'

'I still don't even know what this is all about!' Amy exclaimed. 'What's the case? Who are we saving now? Is this for the golfballs?'

'No, it's Face's old flame,' Hannibal joked. 'He wants us to chauffeur him on a reunion date.'

'Where?' Amy wondered.

'Don't ask,' Hannibal told her.

EIGHTEEN

A DC-10 filled the air with the rumbling of its lift-off and sent its massive shadow sweeping across the neighbourhood surrounding the airport. When the plane passed over the A-Team's van, BA glanced up from the wheel and snickered at the sight of the retreating aircraft. He was in such a good mood because he wasn't on the plane. The others, though, particularly Peck, weren't amused. They sat in stony silence as BA drove away from the airport.

'It isn't funny, BA,' Peck complained.

'Oh, yes it is,' BA chortled. 'You've scammed so many airplanes around here that everybody in town's on to you. Now you can't get within a mile of a plane or even an airport without someone sounding the alarm. That means we can't fly anymore!'

BA let loose with another raucous burst of laughter and thumped his fist on the steering wheel.

'You know, guys,' Amy ventured from the back seat, 'I hate to spoil your thirst for feats of derringdo, but instead of trying to steal a plane, why don't we just buy airline tickets and go as regular passengers?'

'*You* could,' Murdock told her, 'but none of us can get passports. We are persona non grata... sort of like golfballs...'

'And "steal" is an awfully harsh word, Amy,' Hannibal said, clipping the tip off a fat Dutch Masters before lighting it up. 'We like to think in terms of "creative borrowing".'

'Don't matter what you call it, Hannibal,' BA cackled, 'No way we're flyin' this time! Man, I never thought I'd be so jazzed about strikin' out on a scam!'

'Well, could you rub it in a little more gently, BA?' Peck asked him. 'None of the rest of us are looking forward to spending the next week trying to get there by land or sea.'

BA laughed again. ' Maybe we oughta cancel the whole gig, then, eh? Be fine by me.'

As he puffed on his cigar, Hannibal worked his mental gearbox, trying to come up with a new solution for an old problem. A fresh option came to him and he pointed out the window, saying, BA, pull over to that gas station I want to use the phone.'

'Sure thing, Hannibal,' BA said, wrestling with the wheel to make the turn. 'You gonna call Greyhound and book us on a bus to Equador?'

Over BA's laughter, Hannibal muttered, 'Something like that.'

The gas station was one of the few in the whole county selling gas for less than a buck a gallon, and from the looks of the shifty-eyed attendant watching the van from inside the office, one might have concluded he could afford to offer low prices because he routinely lined his pockets by exploiting unwary motorists. BA steered away from the pumps and parked near the two phone booths at the far end of the station.

'I got a full tank, and I don't like the looks of that dude inside,' BA said.

'Well, I won't take long,' Hannibal said, getting out of the van. 'Just sit tight and wait for me.'

Peck didn't feel like waiting. He slipped out the side and confronted Hannibal as he was putting money into one of the phones. 'Who are you gonna call? What's the plan?'

'I'm gonna get us a plane,' Hannibal said matter-of-factly, taking a scrap of paper from his wallet and dialling the number written on it. 'You just be ready with the injection for BA and leave the rest to me.'

'I don't get it,' Peck said. 'I thought we already tried every scam and connection we knew.'

'So did I,' Hannibal said. 'But I was wrong. We got ourselves a trump card just waiting to be used.'

'I still don't get it.'

Hannibal had pulled a handkerchief out of his rear pocket, and he wadded it up to cover the phone's mouthpiece, then altered his 'voice even further when someone answered on the other end of the line. 'Hello, may I speak to Colonel Decker, please?'

'Decker?' Peck gasped, his eyes bulging with wonder. 'Are you nuts, Hannibal?'

'Shhhhhhh,' Hannibal snapped, cupping his hand over the mouthpiece. 'Don't blow this before I even get it off the ground.'

'Come on, Hannibal! Colonel Decker's even more determined to get us behind bars than Colonel Lynch was! We've managed to shake him off our trail for a good month, and now you're calling the guy up and *I'm* the one who's blowing it?' Peck threw his hands up. 'You've gone off –'

Hannibal cut Peck short with a curt wave of his hand, indicating that he'd got through to their most recent arch-nemesis in the military. 'Colonel Decker?' he barked in what passed for his imitation of George C. Scott imitating General Patton. 'This is General Randolph Stratton, Army Intelligence. I've just apprehended the A-Team in their van and we're heading north on one-seventy... yes, you heard correctly, Colonel. We got the whole batch of 'em bundled up in the back of the van here, ready for dispatch to Washington, DC. Now, I want a military transport waiting for us at Brandon Air Field as soon as possible. We're on our way... Colonel, after waiting all this time to catch these guys, I'd think you'd be the last guy wanting to get bogged down with regulations and red tape we might loose 'em through. Look, grease the skids and get a plane ready and on the runway for us by the time we're there. My men and I will do the rest. Don't screw up and we'll find a way for you to get some credit for the apprehension!'

Hannibal hung up the phone and puffed his cigar back into life as he grinned at Peck, who was still in a state of shock. 'Hannibal, I think you're bucking for Murdock's old room in the nut bin. There's no way we'll be able to pull this off!'

'Hey,' Hannibal said jovially, draping an arm across

Peck's shoulder and leading him back to the van. 'You want to see Leslie or not?'

'The only way I'm gonna see her now is if she flies up to visit me in the stockade,' Peck muttered dejectedly.

'Hey, snap out of it, Lieutenant! Listen, we have a mission before us, and you'll quit your damn sulking and lend a hand, it'll be a piece of cake!'

'If you say so.' Face didn't sound convinced. 'I'll get an injection ready for BA.'

'That's the spirit!'

BA was still in jovial mood when Peck and Hannibal returned to the van and got inside. He chuckled, 'So, how we goin', Hannibal? Bus or boat?'

'Neither,' Hannibal said, 'We're goin' by car. I just called an agency that hires out folks to drive other people's new cars cross-country. In this case, we got the option on taking the Ecuadorian consul's new Lincoln all the way down to South America.'

'No kiddin'?' BA said. 'Is that for real?'

'Absolutely. We just gotta get on one-seventy north to be on our way to the agency.'

'You sure you aren't jivin' me?' BA said, suddenly suspicious.

'BA, trust me,' Hannibal said. 'You'll be travellin' as comfortable as you can get...'

NINETEEN

'Aren't we at least going to stop back at the apartment to pack?' Murdock wondered.

'And what about money?' Amy said. 'What are we going to do about money?'

'Hey, relax,' Hannibal told them, 'Face is footing the bill with that advance money he got from the people whose place he was going to redecorate next month. And we've got everything packed here that we'll need. This is a business trip, not a vacation cruise.'

They were headed north on the Hollywood Freeway, also known as Highway 170. As they headed out of the San Fernando Valley, the roadway merged with the Golden State Freeway, also known as Interstate Highway 5. Welcome to Los Angeles, mapmaker's dream and motorist's nightmare. Peck had taken over the driving chores from BA, who was dozing in the back of the van, lured to sleep by the lullaby of sodium pentathol. Amy and Murdock were sitting on either side of him.

'He really does look peaceful when he's asleep,' Amy said, noting the blissful expression on BA's face.

'At least this time he went out with a smile on his face,' Peck said, switching lanes to pass a semi. 'I never thought I was gonna be able to give him that injection.'

'That was a cute trick, saying we all had to be innoculated against... what was that you called it?'

'Hefa Flue Syndrome,' Peck said, '"The scourge of the Tropics." Highly contagious.'

'Not to mention highly fictitious,' Amy countered. 'What was in the shots you gave us?'

'B vitamins,' Peck explained. 'Oughta perk you guys up.'

'Right,' Murdock yawned.

Once out of the valley, the team continued to head north, into the relatively uninhabited area outside the county line, which was divided between barren land, rolling farm plots, and testing-grounds used by all branches of the Armed Service. The smog thinned out, leaving the air clear and the sky a shade of deep blue, streaked here and there by pennant-like cirrus clouds.

'What did you tell the folks at the paper?' Hannibal asked Amy.

'Just that I was checking out a tip on a new story,' she told him. 'It's got to the point where as long as I file good copy, they aren't going to get on my case about keeping regular hours. If need be, I'm sure I can write off a few things we might need as business expenses, too.'

'You're just what this team has always needed, kid,' Hannibal said. 'Someone with looks, brains, and a line of credit.'

'I'm flattered.'

Rounding a wide corner, Peck drove past the first signs of a military presence, a tank going through manoeuvres in a dried-out riverbed surrounded by a twelve-foot high wire fence. Off in the distance, a troop transport helicopter was rising into the air above a series of buildings made out of corrugated steel and cinder block.

'I'm getting a bad case of *deja vu,* Hannibal,' Murdock said, peering through the windshield. 'Don't you think we're playing with fire here?'

'Oh, I don't know about that,' Hannibal replied, puffing contentedly on his cigar. 'I mean, the last place the military would be looking for us is in their own backyard, right?'

'Sheesh,' Peck groaned under his breath as he continued driving past the compound. There was a gateway in the fence at one point, and as the van rolled by, a trio of dark olive sedans spurted out onto the road, sounding their sirens and flashing their rooflights as they closed in on the van.

'Uh, Colonel,' Murdock said, turning to look out through the rear windows of the van. 'Those look like MPs back there, and I don't think they're making all that racket because somebody got married.'

'I wonder if it's Decker,' Amy gasped with alarm.

'Damned if I know,' Hannibal commented, dislodging an inch of smoked residue from his cigar into the dashboard ashtray.

Peck sighed and stepped on the accelerator, lunging the van forward. 'I guess this is where we try to make a run for it, right, Hannibal?'

As they sped towards the main entrance of the base, Hannibal pointed out of the window at the airfield, where a small jet was being readied on the runway. 'Hey, will you take a look at that? Transportation! Come on, Face, let's try the old 'Stick-Our-Heads-In-The-Lion's-Mouth' ploy.'

'Funny, somehow I knew you were going to suggest that.'

As Face pulled further ahead of the pursuing sedans and bore down on the main gate, Hannibal looked back at Amy and Murdock. 'Get ready to transfer BA outta here, along with any essentials we might need for the trip. Murdock, reach into that road kit and hand me a safety flare, wouldja?'

At the main entrance, several armed soldiers were standing guard before a barricade of oversized wooden sawhorses. Having already received word from Colonel Decker to expect the van, they scrambled to clear the way for the A-Team as soon as they turned off the main road. Peck was going too fast, though, and the guards had to dive clear as the van rammed through the barrier, sending splinters of wood flying.

'I'm glad BA wasn't awake to see that,' Peck said, veering onto the tarmac of the runway. 'I think I just put a few dents into his new front end.'

'He'll be lucky if that's all that happens to this heap,' Hannibal said. 'I got a feeling Decker's going to impound it and take his frustrations out on it after we give him the slip.'

'Give him the slip?' Amy wailed. 'It looks to me like we're dropping ourselves in his lap.'

'Cursed be thou of little faith,' Hannibal intoned as they drew up close to the jet, where another group of soldiers were standing at attention, expecting the arrival of a certain

General Randolph Stratton. 'Good, good. This plan is starting to come together now.'

'Plan?' Amy said. 'You call this a plan?!! You'd have made a great kamikaze, Hannibal, that's all I can say.'

Seeing the men around the jet saluting, Hannibal whispered to the others, 'Okay, be ready to move . . . fast!'

Swinging his door open, Hannibal lit the road flare with his cigar. In the few seconds it took to sputter to life, he stepped out and returned the officers' salutes. By the time they realized that the A-Team had arrived without the General, the others were out of the van.

'Grenade,' Hannibal said nonchalantly, tossing the flare in the direction of the men. An acrid cloud of smoke bloomed from the stick with the numbing speed of a self-inflating rubber raft. As the uniformed men scattered from the proximity of the jet, Amy and Murdock scurried up the steps leading into the aircraft while Peck and Hannibal quickly moved around the back of the van, throwing open the doors and dragging BA out. The wind was in their favour, providing a thick enough smokescreen to keep the officers and the arriving MPs from taking potshots at the trio as they struggled up into the hold. By then, Murdock was in command of the cockpit, flicking switches and checking gauges in preparation for takeoff.

'All aboard?' he called out over his shoulder.

'Yes!' Hannibal grunted, easing BA to the floor of the plane and shoving the rolling staircase away from the door so he could close it. 'Let's split, pronto!'

'You got it, Colonel,' Murdock said. Lapsing into a more soothing tone of voice, he called out, 'Equador Airlines Flight 169 now departing. We hope you have a pleasant ride.'

As the jet swung about and taxied down the runway, slowly picking up speed, bullets began to ping off its metallic sides.

'Maybe there was a wedding,' Murdock muttered to himself. 'Somebody's throwing rice.'

'Quit gabbing and start flying, Murdock!' Hannibal ordered.

Murdock lined the jet up on the runway and let loose with the engines. The aircraft surged forward with a loud roar, leaving the snipers behind. Halfway down the runway, the wheels lost touch with the ground and the A-Team was airborne.

'Ta da!' Hannibal cheered. 'I told you I'd get us a plane.'

Amy and Peck were considerably less enthusiastic. Peck glanced down at BA and said, 'I think next time I'll try flying his way . . .'

TWENTY

As far south as the tip of the Baja Peninsula, the A-Team stayed in sight of land, but as the day progressed, Murdock eased the jet out further over the ocean and the coastline fell from view. Everywhere they looked, those aboard the aircraft could see only shades of blue, from the sky's azure brilliance to the dark and brooding hues of the sea. The distant horizon divided the two planes of colour, and even that line was indefinite, appearing not so much like a tight seam as a vague membrane borrowing tints from both. The sun rode its arched path across the sky to their right, and when it finally began to approach the end of its daily jaunt, an inky darkness began to spread through the heavens, revealing stars that had been there all along, waiting for their chance to shine.

In the cockpit, Murdock lorded it over the controls with the assistance of his pet golfball, which had been co-pilot and was resting in the seat next to Murdock, a pair of headphones straddling its trademark.

'I'm telling ya, GB,' Murdock chatted, 'I think the Third World's the right place for us to start our movement. Down there the climate's always right for revolution. All we gotta do is tap in to the public fervour and we'll get things off the ground ... oh, sorry, GB, bad choice of words ...'

While Murdock was engaged in his high-spirited conversation with the golfball, the talk in the main quarters of the plane was more subdued. As BA snored on in the background, the others tried planning ahead for what they'd do once they'd reached the mainland.

'The guy I talked to in the travel office said he couldn't

confirm that there even *is* a Santa Maria's Orphanage in Cayambe,' Amy was saying. 'It's not listed.'

'That doesn't mean much,' Hannibal said. 'That's just where the package was postmarked from. My guess is that the orphanage is tucked away in one of the neighbouring villages or townships.'

Hannibal unfolded a map and set it out before them. As he and Amy looked it over, Peck sat nearby, too preoccupied with his thoughts to participate in the planning.

'Looks like a lot of ground to cover,' Amy said, running a finger over the landscape depicted on the map. 'We might have to rent a car. If Cayambe has any of the major rental outfits, I can get us a discount through the paper.'

'It doesn't matter, Amy,' Peck suddenly blurted out, 'We'll *buy* a car if we have to. I don't care! Whatever it takes, we'll do it!'

Hannibal and Amy glanced at each other as Peck stared back out the window, taking a deep breath to bring himself under control. It didn't seem to work.

'Wanna talk about it, Face?' Hannibal said gently.

Peck gave his head a terse shake, refusing to meet Hannibal's gaze.

From the cockpit, the sound of singing began to fill the air:

> 'Come on boys,
> Let me tell you a tale
> Let me tell you a tale
> 'bout the old Chisolm Trail
> Come a ti-yi-yippee
> Come a ti-yi-yippee
> Come a ti-yi-yippee-yippee-yay...'

'What now?' Amy murmured. 'Don't tell me Murdock's trying to teach his golfball how to sing.'

'He couldn't have any worse luck than he did with Lin,' Hannibal said, getting up. 'Just the same, I think I'll go try to quiet him down before he wakes up Sleeping Beauty.'

Amy waited until Hannibal had stepped around BA and moved into the cockpit, then sat down in the chair across from Peck. Once she was sure she had his attention, she said, 'You know, I'm not used to seeing this side of you... well, actually, I've never seen this side of you.' Getting no response out of Peck, she laughed nervously and continued, 'I mean, ever since I've known you, you've always had a different bombshell on your arm, so I never really thought any one woman could have much of an effect on you. But then, maybe this Leslie Becktall's a differ –'

'She's the only woman I ever loved, you know.' Peck interrupted.

'Oh.'

They were both silent a moment. In the cockpit, Murdock abruptly ceased his singing and could be heard discussing with Hannibal the possible choices for an anthem that would best capture the goals of the Golfball Liberation Army. Peck took another deep breath, then let down his reserve and bared his past to Amy, speaking in a faraway voice.

'She was wonderful,' he recalled, 'Smart. Feisty and fun once you got her out of her shell. The greatest girl I've ever known . . . nothing personal, Amy.'

'No offence taken,' Amy said. 'I figure around here I'm just one of the guys. Go on . . .'

'She could be bright and cheerful, like I said, but she also had this kinda mysterious air about her . . . as if underneath all the laughter, there was something real secretive and precious to her. I found it mesmerizing.'

Amy saw a wistful expression on Peck's face, and, in his eyes, a mingling of nostalgia and sorrow. 'What happened?'

Peck reached into his coat pocket and took out the jewellery box with the fraternity pin. He pried the lid open and stared at the pin as he explained, 'When my graduation was only a few months off, I decided to give her this . . . kind of a pre-engagement gift. You know, it was kind of a custom around the frats and sororities, and it seemed like the right thing to do. I wanted it to be a surprise, so I waited around for the right opportunity. Valentine's Day. There was a big dance and party, sorta like the prom, with fancy clothes and whatnot. I went to her dorm that night to pick her up, but . . .'

When Peck didn't continue, Amy guessed, 'She wasn't there?'

Peck nodded, wrestling with the memory. He tried to

resume talking a few times, but had to stop because his voice was cracking. Finally he was able to go on. 'She'd left school. Her best friend came downstairs and told me Leslie was sorry, but she couldn't see me anymore. That was it, here today, gone tomorrow. No other explanation. She was gone for good and I never found out why.' Peck closed the lid and gave off a bitter laugh. 'I made her friend take the pin ... I couldn't look at it anymore. She must have given it to Leslie. Later on, someone said she'd gone off with another guy. By then it didn't matter why she'd left, only that she had.'

When she realized Peck was finished, Amy leaned over and placed a hand on her friend's arm. 'I'm sorry, Face.'

'You wanna know something funny? Funny and ironic?' Peck said. 'Yesterday afternoon, after I scammed that decorating deal in the bar, I saw this brunette that looked a little like Leslie. I mean, a lot like Leslie. I couldn't believe it. I tracked her down and asked her out. You couldn't believe how charged up I got about it ... I had this idea that maybe I'd be able to recapture some of that old magic, pretend it was Leslie ...'

'And this is why you wanted the penthouse suite to yourself last night?' Amy said.

Peck blushed and nodded. 'Well, it was a basically nice time, but this woman just wasn't Leslie and no amount of pretending was going to change that. Now, the ironic part is, just when I was starting to decide that I might as well enjoy this Gayle for who she was, that's when Father O'Malley came by with the pin and the letter from Leslie. Now, is that weird or what?'

'Whew!' Amy sighed. 'That must have been some blast from the past, huh?'

'You're telling me. Poor Gayle. First I gave her the bum's rush, then she got the place she was staying at drilled with a machine gun by Angel's goons.'

The cockpit door swung open and Hannibal rejoined the others, leaving Murdock to work at improvising on the lyrics of a recent Broadway musical to come up with his new anthem, 'Don't Cry For Me, Little Golf Ball.'

'So how's things going out here?' Hannibal asked.

'Fine,' Amy said.

'And you, Face?'

'I'm doing okay, too, Hannibal.'

Sitting down, Hannibal said, 'Well, Murdock figures we should be in Ecuador by sunup, so we might as well turn in for now, don't you think?'

As Hannibal adjusted his chair so that he could lie back slightly, Peck said, 'I know you all must think I'm stupid for insisting on this expedition, but I *know* Leslie's in trouble. I can feel it. And no matter what happened in the past, I can't just let go of her now.'

'Don't worry about it, Face,' Hannibal assured him. 'The team's behind you a hundred percent.'

BA snored loudly and shifted onto his side.

'Make that eighty percent,' Amy drawled.

TWENTY-ONE

Templeton Peck was right. There was trouble at the Santa Maria Orphanage. Big trouble.

Although the skies were clear over the Pacific, the highlands surrounding Cayambe were in the grip of a squall. Thunder shook the hills and lightning raked the rain-streaked skies with skeletal fingers. The downpour pelted small homes scattered across the countryside and turned dirt roads into quagmires of mud. The courtyard of the Missione Santa Maria was filled with puddles that widened by the minute and drained into one another, forming lakes in the dirt. Dreary as the night was, however, there emanated from within the schoolroom of the nearby orphanage a steady chorus of boisterous cries and rowdy song. It was the sound, not of singing children, but of drunken men. There were five of them, a melting-pot of ethnic dregs, men conditioned to a life outside the law, a life centred around fulfilling gratifications of the moment, at any cost. If their carousing frayed the nerves of those who ran the orphanage and frightened the children who cowered in the beds down the hall, it was of no consequence to them. They had made this place their home, and they were determined to use it as they saw fit.

Marcos and Sanchez were from Cuba, lean, olive-skinned refugees from the law-enforcers of no less than three nations. They were brothers, so similar in appearance that Sanchez wore a bandolier of gun cartridges to distinguish himself from Marcos. Bantu was a tall, broad-shouldered African who'd escaped from the local prison in Cayambe, where he was being held for the murders of two men who had once been his partners in crime. The lone American, Swain, was dishevelled by nature, a loose-limbed loser who'd drifted from country to country, one step ahead of extradition, before linking up with his fellow thugs a month ago. And Gibbens, second in command of the motley crew, hailed from Australia, where he'd been weaned on rustling before striking out across the Pacific to try his hand at smuggling cocaine out of Colombia. A botched deal had resulted in the execution of his compatriots in that scheme, and it had been through a mere quirk of fate that he had been spared the same grisly end. He'd been hiding out in Ecuador since then, waiting for the men who had killed his partners to be given a taste of their own medicine, before returning north. For most of the time, he'd lived in a state of persistent inebriation, and it wasn't until tonight that he had had to face up to the prospect of forced sobriety.

'Gimme another bottle!' he babbled, hurling the fifth he'd just finished across the room. It shattered against the aged adobe wall and at the same time a peal of thunder rattled the roof over their heads. The others found the coincidence to be the stuff of high humour, and they laughed even louder as Gibbens lurched about the centre of the room, overturning several desks as he hollered, 'I want more!'

'There ain't no more!' Swain sniggered playfully. 'We're out!'

'Noooo!' Enraged, Gibbens wrenched the top off a desk and beat it against his forehead until he managed to split it in half. 'No no no!'

'Yes yes yes!' Marcos shouted, giving Gibbens a shove that sent the Australian staggering into the blackboard behind him. Gibbens rebounded and fell upon the Cuban, dragging him to the floor. What their fight lacked in conviction, it made up for in destruction. Up one aisle and down the other they fought, cheered on by their cohorts, using anything and everything within reach as a potential weapon. Erasers, crayon boxes, rulers, and notebooks became instruments of torture in the hands of the wrestling desparados.

The fury of the storm might have drowned out the ruckus in the blassroom for anyone riding by the mission, but inside the orphanage the noise carried down two hallways to the cramped room that Leslie Becktall called home. She fidgeted in bed, trying to shut out the cacophony from her mind as she had so many nights before, but tonight she was too troubled to ignore it any further. Throwing off her covers, she bounded out of bed and slipped a flannel housecoat over her nightgown as she left her bedroom and headed down the hallway. Halfway to the classroom, she ran into an elderly woman in the habit of a nun, who looked as if her mission was the same as Leslie's. They acknowledged each other silently and walked together to the classroom.

Marcos and Gibbens had stopped fighting each other, and all five of the men were taking out their frustration over the absence of strong drink on the desks, stomping on their already-flimsy frames and ripping them apart with their bare hands. Sanchez was the first to spot the two women, and he leered at them as he dropped a chair and propped his thumbs inside his bandoliers the way bankers in the days of old used to fondle their suspenders. 'Well, what a surprise!' he sneered in a crude American accent. 'Would you lovely ladies care to join us *hombres*, huh?'

Leslie and the nun let Sanchez and the other men indulge themselves in a round of lecherous laughter. Then, in an even voice, the older woman told them, 'The noise is waking up the children.'

Gibbens looked at the nun with genuine surprise, but as soon as he turned his head and saw Swain, he couldn't help but break out laughing again. 'The Mother Superior says the noise is waking the children, Swain. Whattaya think o' that?'

'No it ain't, sweetheart,' Swain told the woman. 'Kids love noise, don't you know that?'

Lacking the Mother Superior's restraint, Leslie pointed to the devastated surroundings and railed at the men, 'You've destroyed the classroom! Just look at this place! It's bad enough you have to keep us –'

'Quiet!' the older woman snapped, eyeing Leslie harshly. 'We don't need additional noise from you, child!'

'Aw, don't shut her up!' Gibbens said, sauntering up to Leslie. 'I like her when she's mad.'

125

The Australian reached out and rubbed the back of his hand against the softness of Leslie's face, all the while licking his lips suggestively. Leslie retaliated by ramming her elbow as hard as she could into Gibben's side, banging him with so much force that he howled in pain and doubled over. Furious, he pitched forward in a feeble attempt to tackle Leslie to the floor, but ended up on his knees instead. Even the Mother Superior could no longer stand by passively. When Leslie drove her knee into Gibeen's face and sent him sprawling across the floor, the nun held her back from following through with more blows.

'Now yer done it!' Gibbens roared, dabbing at the blood trickling from the corner of his mouth. He waited for Marcos and Sanchez to come over and lift him up, then the three of them moved forward, closing in on the two women, who shrank back into the corner behind them. Marcos removed a twelve-inch Bowie knife from his boot and his brother began stripping off his bandoliers in anticipation of what he planned to do with Leslie and the nun.

Before any of the men could lay a hand on the caretakers of the orphanage, however, a single gunshot exploded behind them and they stopped where they were. Their eyes slowly turned in the direction the shot had been fired from, and they saw a sixth man standing between Swain and Bantu, leaning on a pair of makeshift crutches as he lowered his pistol. Like the two brothers, Salvador was a Cuban, but he was also the commander of this renegade band, and even though he was visibly ravaged by the effects of a tropical illness, he struck an imposing figure and earned the immediate attention of his men.

'Leave the women alone,' he whispered hoarsely, his voice racked with pain. Rivulets of feverish sweat beaded his forehead, and several drops trailed down his face as he stared at Gibbens and the two Cuban brothers until they followed his orders and backed away from Leslie and the Mother Superior. 'Everyone goes to bed,' he announced with an air of finality. 'Now! There will be no more noise. The children aren't the only ones who want to sleep.'

There was a lingering tension in the classroom as the men

traded glances with one another and the two women. For a moment, it seemed as if Gibbens was about to act in defiance of Salvador's orders, but he finally trudged off to one of the back rooms, consoling himself with a fainthearted kick of the closest desk. The others shuffled off as well, leaving Salvador alone in the classroom with the women.

'Thank you,' the Mother Superior said quietly.

'Go to bed,' Salvador responded before turning around and limping on his crutches back into the room he had emerged from moments before. Over his shoulder, he added, 'Tomorrow you and the children will clean up.'

As Leslie followed the Mother Superior back down the hallway leading to their rooms, she sidestepped a puddle caused by a leak in the ceiling and said, 'How can you thank that man? When are you going to stop letting them control our lives?'

The older woman turned on Leslie and declared, 'When I am no longer responsible for the safety of twenty homeless children who have nothing in life except this place and us. Then, perhaps I would consider your militant approach to peace.'

'Militant?' Leslie protested. 'We're prisoners! They won't even let us fix our leaky roof...!'

They had reached the nun's quarters. She stepped out of the hall and started to close herself inside her room. 'Goodnight,' she told Leslie. 'If you want to do something productive, you might try praying. That is certainly what I intend to do.'

Even after the door had closed on her, Leslie remained in the same place, her superior's words stinging her ears. 'I *have* prayed,' she whispered under her breath. 'I've done more than prayed, more than I should have.'

A rumble of thunder pounded the night air, and Leslie hurried back to her room and threw herself on her bed. Pent-up emotion finally found an outlet, and she wept long and hard with her face buried in her pillow, as if she were trying to blot out the desperate reality that had transformed the orphanage from a place of harmony and hope into a small-scale version of hell. When she had run out of tears, Leslie turned over and lay on her back. As she stared at the ceiling, her hand reached to the nightstand next to the bed and pulled open the drawer. Inside was an envelope, yellowed with age and wear. She picked it up and opened it, removing the equally faded newsclippings that were kept inside. One of the clippings contained a picture of a man in his early twenties, grinning confidently out at the world.

'Oh, Templeton,' she murmured as she stared at the picture. 'Oh, Templeton, what am I going to do?'

TWENTY-TWO

The jet that the A-Team had commandeered for their flight
to Ecuador had been a marvel of modern technology, true
'state-of-the-art' transportation. By contrast, after they
landed in the foggy, rain-soaked fields outside Cayambe the
following dawn, the group changed over to a vehicle more
than a few steps down the ladder of technological evolution.
After an extensive bartering session with a toothless
entrepreneur at the local used car lot, Peck had secured the
use of a Chevy Bel-Air that had come off the assembly line
the same year he'd been born. The bulky four-door looked as
if it hadn't been in contact with a mechanic since then, and
the previous night's rain had done an ineffective job of giving
the car its first washing in months. Dirty streaks lined the
faded blue exterior, giving it a zebra-like appearance that
was accented by the musty, ringed tail of a raccoon tacked to
the antenna. Peck was driving and he sat forward on the edge
of this seat so that he could peer over the spiderweb of cracks
obscuring the lower half of the windshield. Hannibal rode
beside him, bobbing up and down in time with the car's
bounding over ruts and through mudholes on the dirt road
leading to the outskirts of town. He had a map unfolded on
his lap, but, less than a few miles from the used car lot, he'd
already lost track of where they were.

'This map isn't going to do us any good,' he finally said,
folding it up. 'It looks like it was designed for people
travelling by donkey.'

'It *feels* like we're travelling by donkey,' Amy complained
in the back seat as she clung to the nearest arm-rest for
support. 'I'm going to need travel-sickness pills soon.'

'File all complaints with the client,' Hannibal declared, seeking solace in a cigar. 'The cheap client, I might add.'

'I'm just being economical,' Peck said.

'I still say we should have tried to track down a rental place,' Amy said. 'I get this strange paranoia when I'm riding in something that's older than I am.'

'They built cars solidly back then,' Peck defended the Bel-Air. 'This baby was built to last.'

The Chevy testified on behalf of its durability by sputtering noisily under the hood and almost dying on the spot.

'Damned by praise,' Amy smirked.

Looking down the road, Hannibal pointed to a rundown shack with two ancient gas pumps in front and a collection of disabled cars and trucks littering the grounds around it. 'There's a gas station, Face. I know we're not down to fumes yet, but let's splurge and go for another gallon, okay?'

'Very funny,' Peck said.

When the engine went into another fit, Hannibal said, 'Come on, Face, there's probably more condensation in the tank than petrol. Give us all a break and pull in. I didn't bring booties for hiking through mud.'

As Peck reluctantly veered off the road and pulled up to the pumps, Murdock nudged BA and jangled the black man's thirty pounds of gold necklaces. 'Come on, ya little teddy bear! Open those big brown eyes and give us a scowl.' When BA continued to snore, Murdock looked up and lamented, 'I'm worried about him, Hannibal. It's been almost a full day since he and I have insulted each other. I might go into withdrawal soon.'

'Give him time, Murdock,' Peck said. 'We had a long flight, so I had to go heavy on the tranquillizer. It'll wear off soon enough, then we'll be wishing he was back asleep.'

Murdock tried tickling BA's chin and mussing his Mandinka as he made a few faces and tormented his sleeping sidekick with baby talk. 'Coochie-coochie-coo, you little devil you! Time to wake up!' When there was still no response, Murdock retrieved his golfball and tucked it in between BA's ear and the shoulder he was resting his head

130

on. 'You talk to him, GB; give him some rousing rhetoric about the revolution. That'll snap him out of it.'

While Peck got out of the car and tried to figure out how the gas pump worked, Amy and Hannibal tracked down the attendant, who was engrossed with his daily ritual of feeding the cluster of chickens that lived in the rusting shells of the dead autos. He was a portly man with a handlebar moustache and a wide-brimmed hat. Crouched over the chickens, he was talking to them in their own tongue, clucking as if he were about to lay an egg of his own.

'Excuse me, señor,' Hannibal interrupted. 'Do you speak English?'

The attendant rubbed some seed residue off on his pants, then brushed a lock of hair from his eyes as he regarded Amy and Hannibal. 'No,' he said in a faltering voice. 'Not too much.'

'Oh.' Hannibal groaned. 'Okay... uh, well... *Donde está Santa Maria*... uh...' He looked at Amy. 'Do you know how to say orphanage?'

'Casa de niños?' Amy ventured.

'Niños y niñas?' Hannibal elaborated, trying to get a flicker of recognition to register on the Ecuadorian's face. *Santa Maria? Casa?'*

It was all Greek to the attendant. Tipping the brim back on his hat, he scratched his head and shrugged his shoulders. Murdock noticed Hannibal's plight and piled out of the Bel-Air.

'Colonel, let me try,' he said. Clearing his throat, he screwed up his face and spoke to the attendant in tourist Spanish. 'Pleeeeese to excuse, but where ees zee orphanage Santa Maria? We like to be going there.'

'Ah, *si! La orfandad*!' the attendant said, his eyes brightening. Turning slightly, he pointed to the higher elevations stretching out in the distance. 'Up there, in the hills!'

'Gracias!' Murdock replied graciously.

As the group headed back to where Peck was pumping a last few pints of gas into the Chevy, Hannibal leaned close to Murdock and whispered, 'I don't get it. All you did was

131

speak English with a Spanish accent.'

'Yeah, I know. They're used to that, Hannibal,' Murdock explained. 'It's like ... it's what they call dialect! You have to have a certain affinity for the regional inflections and all the little subtle nuances of speech.'

'Right,' Amy muttered, 'You also have to watch a lot of bad telelvision with people talking pidgin Spanish.'

Peck had converted his dollars to pesos back at an exchange shop next to the used car lot, and he peeled off a few bills to pay for the gas. As the attendant made change, he warned the others, 'The seesters, they no like strangers. They only pray. Only want peace.'

'Believe me, we come in peace,' Hannibal said. Behind him, Amy opened the back door of the Chevy, and BA's snoring rolled out like the buzz on an unoiled chain saw. The attendant glanced in at BA and his eyes widened with apprehension. 'He comes in peace, too,' Hannibal insisted. 'Take my word for it.'

Before anyone else got back into the Bel-Air, the drone of another engine cut through the morning air. Peck looked down the road and saw a jeep approaching the station, filled with armed soldiers.

'Looks like trouble, Hannibal.'

Hannibal spotted the jeep and quickly put out his cigar. 'Don't hold me to it, gang, but we may not want to be on display while the *federales* check their oil ... know what I mean?'

Peck slipped the attendant a few more bills and gestured for him to keep quiet about them while Murdock and Hannibal hurriedly dragged BA from the back of the Chevy and followed Amy to the cover of the nearest wrecked autos. They managed to conceal themselves scant seconds before the jeep pulled into the station. An officer riding in the front seat began to talk animatedly with the attendant.

BA's sedative was beginning to wear off. Lying in the dirt, he stirred and began blinking his eyes. As he opened his mouth, Murdock reacted quickly, yanking off his cap and stuffing it between BA's teeth at the same time putting a finger to his lips and whispering, 'Shhhhhh.' The restraining measures only hastened BA's return to consciousness, and his face darkened with anger as he tried to shout something through the hat. Murdock dived on top of the larger man like a wrestler trying to pin an opponent. Peck helped hold down BA's legs.

'Hannibal!' Murdock whispered desperately, 'I can't keep this up long. This is one mean Brahma...'

'Mmmmmmpffffhhh!' BA gargled with fury.

Peering over the hood of the car they were hiding behind, Peck watched the men in the jeep and wondered aloud, 'You think they're looking for us, Hannibal?'

'Seems like a long shot to me,' Hannibal said. 'No sense taking any chances, though.'

'Long shot, huh?' Peck hissed. 'Remember that little jet plane you so cleverly lined up for us out from under the military's nose? I've got a wad of pesos that says any first-week radar school student coulda tracked our flight all the way down here. Hell, Decker could be down at the Cayambe Hilton for all we know, waiting for these goons to serve him up our heads on a platter...'

'Well, it doesn't look like we'll have to worry about that just yet.'

On a hand signal from the ranking officer, the jeep's driver shifted gears and drove off, heading back the way they'd come. The attendant waved to them, then checked his shirt pocket to make sure his bribe was still there before turning and giving the A-Team a thumbs-up. As Hannibal and Peck rose from their crouches, Murdock was suddenly propelled into the air by BA, who was now wide awake and livid. Jerking Murdock's cap from his mouth and wringing it in his massive hands, BA shouted, 'Listen, fool, you feed me your hat again, you ain't gonna have a head to wear it on!'

'Hey, claim down, BA,' Hannibal said. 'What's the matter, you get up on the wrong side of the equator or something?'

'Where are we?' BA sputtered, staring uncertainly at the tropical surroundings. 'How'd we get here? You psychos drugged me again, didn't you?'

'Boy what a grump!' Murdock complained, dusting himself off and catching up with the others, who were

133

heading back to their jalopy. Wagging a finger at BA, he scolded, 'Cranky in the morning; cranky all day.'

Amy pulled a notebook out of her purse and asked Peck, 'Just for our records, what'd you just spend on gas?'

Before Peck could answer, BA pointed an accusatory finger at Murdock and asked Hannibal, 'Did that crazy fool fly us here? Did he fly us to Ecuador?'

'Five bucks' worth,' Peck told Amy, 'in pecos.'

'You didn't get a full tank?'

'It's enough to get us to the orphanage, I'm sure.'

'Mr Extravagance strikes again.'

BA squinted against the first rays of sunlight breaking through the cloudcover and pressed his palms against either side of his head. 'Every time we go on one of these cases, I wake up in a foreign country with a bad headache. I'm tired of it, Hannibal!'

'We all have to pay our price, BA,' Hannibal said, 'Even misers like Face.'

'Hey, if it weren't for the fact that you guys loused up my best two scams, we could be tooling around in a limo now instead of pinching pennies,' Peck reminded them as he handed the car keys to BA, 'Now that you're up, big guy, you can drive.'

BA stood and watched as the others climbed into the Chevy, then ran a finger along the grimy right fender on his way to the driver's seat. Once he'd got in behind the wheel and started up the engine, he promised, 'One of these days I'm gonna pound you people into the ground. I'm gonna stop being a nice guy about this.'

As BA pulled out onto the road heading up into the hills, he heard a slight cackling in the back seat and glared into the rear-view mirror. 'Somebody laughin' at me back there?'

'Not me,' Murdock said.

'Me neither, BA,' Peck said.

'I think there's a chicken here somewhere,' Amy said as she leaned forward in her seat. Sure enough, one of the fowls from the gas station had mistaken the Chevy for the latest in home accommodation and was nuzzled under the front seat. When Amy prodded it with her toe, the bird fluttered out from hiding and squawked raucously as it eluded the three riders in the back seat who were trying to grab it. Murdock was finally able to roll down his window and chase the chicken out. It landed in the mud with a 'splat', then scurried over to the other shoulder, beating its stubby wings frantically.

'Why did that chicken cross the road?' Murdock asked.

'No way I'm gonna touch that one,' Peck said.

BA was still sullen. Wiping dust off the dashboard and snapping the tossles that lined the roof, he said, 'One minute I'm drivin' my shiny van, which I probably ain't gonna even see anymore, and the next minute I'm in Ecuador. It's over. No more. You ain't kicking BA Baracus around no more. This is it. The last time. I've had it!'

'Shut up!' the others cried out in unison.

BA shook his head and guided the Chevy up the next bend, grumbling, 'Man, we better find this Leslie chick, Face, that's all I gotta say.'

'We will,' Peck replied. 'We will...'

TWENTY-THREE

Salvador's temperature dropped slightly during the night, but he retained a considerable fever that burned off more of his strength. Sweat streamed down his face and through the bristle on his unshaved chin. His eyes had a yellowish cast that betrayed the sickness he struggled to ignore. He was lying on a musty cot in the supply room, his body tilted at a slight angle as he supported himself on one unsteady elbow. The morning light shone through a window across the room in a broad beam filled with dancing motes of dust. Through the window, Salvador could see the side of the church and much of the mission courtyard, where clinging vines and other well-tended plants glistened fresh and clean in the aftermath of the rain.

'Please, try to eat some of this,' the Mother Superior was telling him as she held out a tablespoon heaped high with oatmeal. She was seated in a chair next to the cot and in front of the supply shelves, which were stacked with dwindling reserves of canned goods, whole grains, and other storable foods.

Salvador looked at the steamy offering and made a disgusted face as he shoved her hand away. 'Get that slop out of my face!' he retorted, his voice ragged and weak despite his anger.

'You need your strength.'

'You don't care about my strength,' he told her as a twisted smile unfolded across his face. 'You just want me out of here.'

'I admit my concern for your health isn't based entirely on my fondness for you,' the nun confessed as she dipped the

136

tablespoon into the bowl on her lap for a fresh scoop of oatmeal. 'But I try my best to have good feelings for all people, regardless of their shortcomings.'

'Yeah,' Salvador chortled, 'and you better have real good feelings for me, lady, or a lot of faith in that God of yours, because if I don't start getting...' Salvador fell suddenly silent, having heard a bell ring outside the doors to the courtyard. The Mother Superior heard it, too, and rose to her feet to look out as well.

'I'm not expecting anyone,' she said. 'I wonder who it could be?'

With great strain, Salvador reached over and grabbed a revolver from his holster, which hung over a nail at the end of the shelves. He pulled back the hammer and took aim at the nun. 'You know the routine. Get rid of them, Sister. Fast... or you start losing some of your orphans.'

'There's no need for you to point that vile thing at me,' she said as she set aside the bowl and rose from the chair. 'I'm more than familiar with your threats after all these weeks. You can rest assured I won't do anything to jeopardize the safety of my young ones.'

As she left the supply room, the Mother Superior made a swift Sign of the Cross and kissed the crucifix dangling from her neck on a simple gold-plated chain. To leave the orphanage, she had to pass by the activity room, where several of the young children were playing with broken toys and building blocks under the supervision of another nun. She paused a moment to watch the youngsters who were absorbed with their playing and had no conception of the tyranny under which they'd been living for close to a month, since the day Salvador's men first arrived at the orphanage. With the men using the orphanage as their temporary hideout, the Mother Superior had been forced to tell the outside world that an outbreak of contagious measles amongst some of the children had necessitated quarantining the entire mission until further notice. Word had been passed along to the villagers, and there had been fewer and fewer visitors to the mission lately. In fact, this was the first time this week that the bell outside the courtyard gates had been rung.

Although the sun was shining brightly now, the courtyard was still pocked with muddy pools of water from the rain, and the Mother Superior had to raise the hem of her habit so that it wouldn't be soiled as she sought out the driest footing and made her way to the large wooden gates. Raising a thick bolt, she opened the gate just enough to look out at the visitors. Her heart skipped a beat when she saw the A-Team, particularly BA, who she mistook at first for colleagues of Salvador.

'May I help you?' she asked stiffly.

'Uh, yeah,' Peck said, holding his hat in his hands. 'I hope so. We're looking for a woman named Leslie Becktall. She's supposed to work here.'

The nun frowned, then shook her head. 'I'm sorry, but we have no one by that name on our staff. Now, I'll have to ask you to leave. Perhaps you cannot read Spanish, but there is a sign on your side of the gate saying that this area is under quarantine because of a measles breakout. Good day to you.'

When she tried to close the gate, Peck reached out and held it open, insisting, 'But she wrote to me on stationery that had this orphanage's name on it. Now, if I could just–'

'Perhaps it was another orphanage or simply old stationery.' The Mother Superior tried again to shut out the A-Team, but this time Hannibal intervened, asking, 'Could we talk to the other nuns or speak to the children?'

The Mother Superior took a deep breath, then firmly declared, 'We have no one named Leslie Becktall. I'm sorry. Now, please let go of this door and be on your way.'

Peck and Hannibal stepped back and the woman slammed the gate shut.

'Not exactly the "singing Nun", was she,' Hannibal mumbled.

Amy put a hand on Peck's shoulder and apologized, 'I'm sorry, Face.'

Peck stared at the closed gates, unconvinced by what he'd heard from the nun. 'It just doesn't make sense. This is the Santa Maria Orphanage and that's what the letterhead on Leslie's note read. Now could she have got her hands on the stationery if she didn't stay here? And I don't buy this measles epidemic story, either.'

'Well, there's not much we can do about it right now,' Hannibal reflected as the group turned and headed back to the Chevy. 'Maybe if we ask around we can come up with another bead on this thing, then . . . hey, take a look at that!'

In a field of overgrown grass next to the mission, another nun was chasing a young boy who was crying as he ran away from the church and orphanage.

'Enrico!' the woman cried out as her longer strides closed the distance between her and the child.

As he watched the chase, BA mused, 'Doesn't look like anyone wants to stay in this place.'

'Well, at least I can have a chance to talk to someone else around here,' Peck said as he dashed off toward the field. The nun had tripped and fallen in the tall grass as she was about to grap the runaway child, and Enrico raced away from her without looking back. Peck broke into a run and passed the downed nun, overtaking the boy before he could flee into a grove of thick trees. Enrico began to cry and he struggled to get free when Peck picked him up and carried him back to the nun.

'Oh, thank you,' she said as she stood up and brushed loose grass from her habit. 'He always tries to run away when it's time for his bath . . .'

As she reached for the child and made eye contact with Peck, the nun let out an involuntary gasp. Peck's jaw dropped and his eyes widened with disbelief.

'Leslie . . .' he whispered feebly.

Leslie held the child close to her and her jaw quivered as she floundered under the burden of unleashed emotions. She finally managed to respond, 'Templeton?'

It was hard to tell which of the two was the more stunned. They stood silently, staring at one another, bridging the years that had passed since their last meeting. Even young Enrico sensed the tension and fell quiet, holding onto Leslie's hand and looking up at Peck.

'Why are you in that outfit?' Peck asked. Even as the words were tumbling out, he realized their absurdity.

Crestfallen, he sagged from the impact of realization.

'You shouldn't have come here,' Leslie told him. 'You have to leave. Now.'

'Wait a minute!' Peck reached out for Leslie, but she wheeled about and dragged Enrico back towards the side gate to the mission. He began running after them, shouting, 'Wait! Leslie!'

Before Peck could catch up with Leslie, the battered Chevy forged through the deep grass and cut him off. The rest of the A-Team was inside, and Amy threw open the back door for him to get in. 'Hurry, Face, the *Federales* are coming!'

Peck glanced over his shoulder and saw the same jeep they'd spotted at the gas station earlier. It was negotiating its way around pot-holes and mud puddles as it headed toward the mission. 'Damn!' Peck swore as he joined the others and BA sped off into the cover of the nearby grove.

'How did they know to look here?' Murdock said.

'Who knows?' Hannibal replied. 'Maybe the guy at the station had a change of heart and blew the whistle on us after all.'

Once they were in the woods, BA turned off the engine and the team stared through the cluster of trunks at the mission, where the *federales* had come to a halt before the courtyard gates. The officer climbed out and rang the mission bell.

'If the Mother Superior doesn't fink on us,' Hannibal said, 'they'll probably spot the path we made through the grass. BA, I think you better be ready to gun that engine back up and speed out of here.'

Peck's mind was still on his encounter with Leslie. 'I don't believe it. I don't believe it,' he muttered. 'Never in a million years...'

'Now at least you know why no one had heard of Leslie Becktall,' Hannibal said.

As before, the gate to the courtyard opened a little way and the older nun poked her head out. She and the officer traded a few words while another soldier bounded out of the jeep and hammered a poster into place next to the notice regarding the quarantine of the mission.

'I hope you've had a measles shot, Face,' BA said. 'Man, you had your hands all over that kid.'

'He looked healthy to me,' Peck said. 'I'll bet there's nobody with measles in there. She was trying to hide something from me. I don't know what, but I aim to find out.'

'Not right now, you aren't,' Hannibal told him.

Back at the mission, the gate closed and the officer got back in the jeep, along with the other soldier. The jeep backed up but apparently no one had seen the tracks the Chevy had made in the field, because the *federales* headed off in the opposite direction, making their way back toward the city. BA waited until the jeep was out of sight, then started up the engine.

'What we doin' now?' he asked.

'Let's go grab something to eat while we think things through,' Hannibal said. 'This job isn't turning out the way any of us planned...'

TWENTY-FOUR

A couple of miles north of the mission, the A-Team came across a small village with enough visible tourist traps to make them feel comfortable. They sought out a small, quaint cafe tucked away on a side road and sat down on the patio, which had almost completely dried under the persistent rays of the sun. A few mosquitos flitted around a pool of stagnant water at the base of a large shady tree, but none of the insects strayed out onto the patio to menace the diners. Hannibal ordered a pitcher of cold beer and a plate of fresh chips while the others perused the laminated menus. Peck stared vacantly at his menu, his mind elsewhere.

'Tough break, Face,' Hannibal said. 'My guess is your old flame had her name changed to Sister Mary Katherine or something like that after she became a nun. I'm not sure why she sent you that letter, but I get this feeling she wasn't out to rekindle that flame. Sorry, kid.'

'Boy,' Murdock said, 'when they say she ran off with another guy, they weren't kidding.'

Peck set his menu down and shook his head numbly. 'I still can't believe ... can't believe she never said anything while we were dating.'

'Maybe you broke her heart without knowin' it, man,' BA suggested. 'This could be her idea of runnin' of to join the foreign legion.'

'I don't think so.' Peck looked out at the hills that rose behind the village. 'You know, she always had that mysterious side to her. I always thought it was something artistic, like a poet. I mean, I've never known any poets, but I figured they acted the same way, always standing back from everything and looking at it different from everyone else. Who knows, maybe when I thought she was composing poems to herself, she was really praying.'

The chunky proprietor returned to the table with the chips and beer, then took a pad out of his rear pocket to jot down orders. As the others decided what they watned, Hannibal told Peck, 'Well, at least you now know the real story. It ought to make you feel a little better.'

'And it didn't even end up costing you that much,' Amy said, going over the figures in her notebook, then ripping out the expense sheet and handing it to Peck.

'An invoice?' Peck said, glancing at the sheet. He slid it back across the table at Amy, snapping out of his funk. 'Hey, this case isn't over yet! Those nuns are in some kind of trouble. We can't just pack up and go home!'

'Wanna bet?' BA said. 'Gonna take a while to get back since we ain't flyin', and we ain't flyin', right? Right, everybody?'

'Come on, you guys!' Peck said as the proprietor waddled back inside the cafe kitchen area. 'I know Leslie. I recognize the tone in her voice.'

Amy, Murdock, and BA all groaned, but Hannibal was less willing to completely disregard Peck's concern. As he poured himself a beer, he said, 'Okay, look. I can see your point, Face. You might have something...'

'Oh yeah?' BA snarled, 'You recognize the tone in her voice, too, Hannibal?'

'All nuns sound alike to me, BA,' Hannibal countered. 'Suppose, just suppose, that there really isn't a measles outbreak back at the orphanage. What if it's something else that's got that place locked up?'

'Like what?' Amy asked.

'I don't know for sure,' Hannibal said. 'But I think that since we came halfway around the world to check things out, we oughta at least make sure we aren't needed. Look at it this way, if there *was* a measles outbreak there, I still don't think it would make those nuns act so bent out of shape when visitors came by. It's been a while since I've been to church, but I seem to remember that most religious orders are based

143

around being a little more receptive to one's fellow man than the treatment we got.'

'Exactly!' Peck exclaimed. 'But for some reason, those sisters can't talk! I know that if I could just get to Leslie, I could find out what's going on.'

Hannibal took a chip and dipped it into a bowl of spicy salsa. He took two bites of the combination and immediately grabbed for his beer to quell the burning sensation in his mouth. Once the fire was out, he looked at Peck and said, 'If you want to get to Leslie, you're gonna have to go back and get inside the orphanage.'

'I know that!' Peck said, frustrated. 'What am I supposed to do? Tell 'em I'm a health inspector? Show 'em my orphan papers?'

Hannibal shook his head, staring past the patio at the back yard across the street, where laundry was hanging out on a clothesline to dry. Most of the clothes were black, and Hannibal spotted a pair of tall, lean nuns clipping up the laundry. 'What I think you might want to do, Face, is polish up on your rosary.'

'My what?'

'You know the old saying, "When in the nunnery, do as the nuns do."'

Peck noticed where Hannibal was looking and said, 'Oh, come on! It would never work!'

'Now, now, is that any way to talk, Sister Face?'

The others looked across the street, watching the two nuns finish hanging out the wash. Peck said, 'Well, maybe it *could* work. That nun on the right looks about my height.'

'The other one's a little taller and thinner,' Murdock said.

'Just like you, Murdock,' Hannibal said.

'Me, Colonel?'

Hannibal nodded. 'I'd just as soon not have Face try this alone.'

'Who knows, Murdock,' Peck added, 'Maybe you'd get a chance to get your golfball baptized. I'm sure it'd be a must if you're going to try to drum up support in these parts. This here's Catholic country, and I don't think anyone's going to feel much sympathy for an atheist golfball.'

'Yeah, I think you're right, Face,' Murdock conceded, taking the ball from his flight jacket. 'You hear that, GB?'

Once the owner brought out their food, Face and Murdock ate hurriedly, keeping an eye on the nuns across the street. When the two women finished their task, they wandered off into the nearby church.

'Okay, we're on,' Peck said, swallowing down the last of his burrito as he got up from his seat. 'Let's go, Murdock.'

BA had left the keys to the Chevy on the table next to his plate, and Hannibal reached for them, then gave them to Peck, saying, 'You guys drive down and park in those woods next to the mission. We'll hike down after we've rested a few minutes, then wait for you to come out with some info. If we don't see or hear from you by noon, we're coming in after you, whatever it takes.'

Peck nodded, then followed Murdock across the street. They checked to make sure no one else was watching them, then wriggled through the hedge surrounding the church property. The rest of the team couldn't see them for several seconds after that, but then two habits suddenly seemed to jump free of the line, and Hannibal could see Peck and Murdock reach out to catch the outfits before they fell to the ground. Moments later, the two men re-emerged through the hedge and flashed an 'okay' signal before getting into the Chevy and driving off.

On the patio, Hannibal, BA, and Amy finished their meals slowly, none of them saying anything. Amy was the first to speak up afterwards. 'I'm starting to worry, Hannibal. If there's something wrong at the mission, just the two of them might not be able to handle it.'

'Relax, Amy,' Hannibal said as he pushed his plate away and started unwrapping an after-dinner cigar. 'They're just going to do some undercover reconnaissance. If it comes down to action, I'm sure they'll wait until we're there to back 'em up. Everything will be fine.'

'I hope so.'

BA mopped up his plate with a flour tortilla, then chewed it down before saying, 'I just hope Murdock doesn't go off on some crazy trip once he puts on that nun's getup. It'd be just like that fool to start swingin' from the lights and laying his lunatic rap on everyone. Man, the more I think about it, the more I get to thinkin' we shouldn't have let that clown go with Face.'

'He was the only one who'd fit the habit,' Hannibal said.

'I'm sure I could have fitted in it closely enough,' Amy said.

'Yeah, but you don't have ten years of commando experience with Face,' Hannibal reminded her. 'If they run into trouble, they'll be in better shape to deal with it than you and him would have.'

'Maybe so.'

BA was leaning back in his seat and staring idly at the parking lot when he suddenly sat upright and whispered across the table, 'Man, you ain't gonna believe it, Hannibal, we're havin' more trouble shakin' off those *federales* than a dog has shaking off fleas.'

Hannibal looked over, spotting the uniformed officials, who were now conversing with the cafe owner. 'These aren't the same guys we saw before.'

'Yeah, but they're doin' the same thing... lookin' for trouble.'

'Stay calm,' Hannibal said. 'Maybe they aren't looking for us. Not *every* government is after us, you know.'

'I ain't takin' no chances.' BA grabbed his silverware and held it underneath the table, ready for quick use. 'They come after me and I'm gonna slice and dice 'em!'

'I kinda wish we hadn't left all our goodies in the car,' Hannibal said, closing his fingers around his beer bottle. 'I'd feel better with an Uzi in my hand than this. Now, let's just keep cool and wait it out...'

The proprietor nodded in response to a question from the officer he was speaking to, then pointed to the patio. The officer thanked the owner, then headed for the patio, followed by two other soldiers. One of them was carrying a machine gun, the other a hammer and a small poster. At their table, Hannibal, Amy, and BA tried to remain nonchalant while at the same time every fibre in their bodies was braced for the prospect of confrontation. As it turned

146

out, though, the three uniformed men strode past the table without paying any attention to the Americans. They paused before an upright beam supporting the overhead trellis-work, and the soldier with the hammer pounded the poster he'd been carrying onto the beam. The officer straightened the poster, then led his men from the patio and back to their jeep.

'Whewwwwwww!' Hannibal exhaled.

BA brought his silverware back up from under the table and set it down next to his plate. 'That was close, man!'

Amy looked over at the beam and said, 'It looks like they put up a wanted poster. I thought that went out with the Old West.'

'Maybe they don't have a post office here,' Hannibal said as he got up and walked over to take a look at the man depicted on the poster. It was Salvador, and he was wanted for a range of crimes including murder and robbery. There was a price on his head and the government said they'd take him dead or alive. 'Looks like a real friendly guy, doesn't he?'

BA leaned forward to read the small print. 'Says here he runs around with a whole gang of bad news.'

'I'm suddenly getting a very bad feeling,' Amy said.

'Maybe he's the reason the nun's aren't talking,' BA said, putting Amy's fears into words.

'I think it's time we headed back to the mission,' Hannibal said. 'If we can flag a ride, I think we oughta take it. I want to get there as soon as possible...'

TWENTY-FIVE

Twice a week, the parish priest would ride from the village to Santa Maria's to celebrate Mass and hear the confessions of the sisters and orphans. He looked upon his visits as necessary obligations, a penance for those small sins he committed in the line of his duties as a man of the cloth. As such, he did not enjoy either the trips or the time spent at the mission, which had not been open to the public for years. Lacking any sense of empathy for or commitment to the orphanage, it was not surprising that he could have made eight bi-weekly visits over the course of the past month without once suspecting or even sensing that a band of renegade cut-throats were indulging themselves in a reign of terror over those living at the mission. Fearing reprisal, neither the nuns nor the children had spoken a word of their captivity, even in the privacy of the confessional. And so, that morning, as on so many mornings before, the priest completed his services and promptly left the mission through the same rear door to the church through which he had entered. In fact, in all the time he'd acted as the mission's part time priest, he'd never ventured into either the courtyard or orphanage. Salvador could have been training an army at Santa Maria's and the priest would not have known it provided the soldiers stayed away from the church.

With the services completed, the nuns filed out of the side door of the church, immediately encountering an armed guard in the person of Marcos, who gestured with his automatic rifle for the nuns to walk in single file along the sidewalk leading from the church to the orphanage. Marcos had performed the same task without incident countless times before, so his attentiveness was cursory at best, and he failed to notice that the last nun in line was wearing high-top sneakers and that the second-to-last sister's feet were snuggly fitted inside a pair of Gucci loafers.

'So far so good,' Peck whispered over his shoulder to Murdock as they headed for the orphanage. 'I'm glad we were able to sneak in when we did.'

'Next time we do this, Face, let's dress up like priests or gardeners,' Murdock suggested. 'I have enough complexes already without branching out into transvesticism.'

Sanchez and Bantu were smoking cigarettes on the front porch when the nuns returned to the orphanage, and they both leered at the women as they filed past to go inside.

'Did you pray for our souls too, ladies?' Sanchez chuckled.

Leslie was at the head of the line and she whirled about, having heard the remark. She was about to give Sanchez a piece of her mind when she spotted Peck and Murdock at the end of the line, their heads bowed low to avoid recognition. She knew who Peck was immediately, and, blushing, she turned back around and continued into the main building. Once inside, the other nuns dispersed, leaving Leslie alone with the two imposters.

'What are you doing?' she demanded hotly. 'I told you to go, Templeton!'

'We have to talk, Leslie,' Peck insisted, pointing to the room behind them. 'Come on. Murdock, stay out here and keep an eye on things.'

Murdock curtsied mockingly and picked up a broom. He began sweeping the dirt floor as Peck and Leslie stepped into the room and closed the door behind them. By force of habit he began humming to himself, and it wasn't until another of the nuns walked by and cleared her throat discreetly that Murdock realized he was humming 'Sympathy for the Devil'. He quickly changed his tune to 'Silent Night', the closest thing to a religious hymn he could think of.

Several minutes passed, during which Murdock had swept the same area five times, and then there was a sound down the hallway. Salvador was attempting to walk on his crutches, flanked on one side by Gibbens. The gangleader's breathing was laboured, and each step was an ordeal. Salvador's frustration mounted, and when he lost his balance a few feet away from Murdock and slumped to the ground, he lashed out with his crutch, inadvertently knocking the broom from Murdock's hands and sending it flying against the wall.

'Just too early, Sal ol' bean,' Gibbens said as he helped the Cuban to his feet. 'Gotta let this healin' take its course instead o' rushin' things all the time.'

'To hell with it!' Salvador cursed. 'Take me back to my room!'

Murdock had shrunk away from Salvador the moment he'd lost the broom, and he continued to put on the same act until the two men had moved back into the supply room. Then he took a few steps back and rapped his knuckles against the door Peck and Leslie had disappeared behind. 'Let's speed this up, Faceman!' he whispered thorugh the crack in the door.

Inside the room, Peck was removing his disguise as he appealed to his former love. 'Leslie, would you please tell me what's going on here?'

'Theresa,' Leslie corrected him, trying to remain aloof. 'My name is Sister Theresa now.'

Peck stepped out from under the habit, then removed the nun's headpiece and brushed his hair back into place with his palm. 'Okay... Sister Theresa,' he said, cringing at the name. 'Would you explain yourself? I've come a few thousand miles to see you, so I think you owe me that much, don't you? I won't even get into the explanations you owe me from half a lifetime ago...'

Leslie bit her knuckles nervously, losing the battle to control her emotions. 'If I'd known you would come, I would never have written,' she said, unable to look Peck in the eye. 'I just felt as if everything here might be coming to an end... that maybe I needed to tie up some loose ends in case something happened to me.'

'I see,' Peck said with a trace of bitterness. 'That's what I am to you, huh? A loose end?'

Leslie turned and faced Peck. 'You were the biggest loose

end of my life . . . because I cared so much about you . . . and still do. I just didn't want you to think that my leaving school the way I did meant that I'd lost any feeling for you. In fact, it was just the other way around . . . I didn't want to admit that there were doubts about my decision and . . . does any of this make sense to you?'

Peck moved closer to Leslie, swallowing hard. 'Yes, I understand. But why did it have to wait this long? Why didn't you tell me about this fifteen years ago? It would have been so much easier on both of us. Do you know what you did to me? Do you have any idea what kind of scars I've had on my heart since you walked out of my life without a word? Do you?'

Leslie blinked several times, then closed her eyes tightly. The tears streamed out anyway, and she finally threw herself into Peck's uncertain embrace and sobbed, 'I'm so sorry, Templeton. I'm so, so sorry.'

'That makes two of us,' Peck responded, fighting back his own tears. He couldn't remember the last time he'd been so much at the mercy of his emotions.

When she had spent her first volley of tears, Leslie pulled herself away from Peck and sniffled, 'I wanted to tell you then, but I knew if I met with you one more time, I wouldn't have gone ahead with my plan to be a nun.'

'Would becoming Mrs Templeton Peck have been such a bad second choice?' he asked her, only half teasing.

'It would have been a wonderful second choice,' Leslie admitted. 'But, after a while, I would have known that it *was* the second choice, not the first.'

'That's fine,' Peck snapped, turning his back on Leslie and pacing to the other side of the room. 'At least I know where I stand.'

Leslie sighed with the resignation of one who's divulged a secret against their better judgement and come to regret it. 'I don't expect anyone to understand any of this,' she said, 'but, somehow, Temp, even after all the pain I've caused you, and the torment I've suffered over the decision . . . when I'm in that church, or think of the vows I've taken and the things I've accomplished as a nun, everything in this ridiculous world makes sense to me. It gives meaning to my life. Can't you accept that and be glad for me?'

Peck paused before the window and stared out at the midday sky, battling to put the revelations of the past few hours into some sort of manageable perspective. Nothing had turned out the way he'd hoped, apart from the fact that he'd found Leslie alive and healthy. All along, he had nurtured the hope that his quest would be rewarded with a reunion with Leslie that might have led to a resumption of their romance and its logical fulfilment. Now those hopes had been shattered, and he was being asked to be happy for the woman who'd just broken his heart a second time. He didn't have much of a choice, to his way of thinking. He finally turned back to Leslie and nodded. 'I understand,' he muttered, 'and I wish you all the best.'

Before Leslie could express her gratitude, Murdock suddenly sprang into the room, almost tripping over the hem of his habit as he interrupted them. 'I hate to butt in, groovy guys and gals, but activity is starting to pick up out here. The goons with the guns are saying something about a head count...'

'Twice a day they count the Sisters and children to make sure no one has escaped,' Leslie explained. 'They started doing it after I sneaked one of the kids out through an old tunnel in the wine cellar. He's the one who saw to it that my package got mailed to you, Templeton.'

'Thanks, kid, wherever you are,' Peck said.

'Excuse me, ma'am,' Murdock said to Leslie, 'but could you tell me whose those guys are? They don't seem like the religious type.'

'They're a pack of jackals that came down from the hills one day and never left,' Leslie divulged. 'They're wanted for a variety of crimes and their leader was badly wounded in a shootout before they arrived. We took the bullet out but he's been fighting infection ever since. They're hiding from the *federales* until he recuperates.'

'Have they done anything here?' Peck stammered, 'I mean, to the children... to you?'

'Not so much to us as the furnishings. They take their

anger out by destroying things. It's frightening for the kids, though. The men get drunk almost every night and ravage another room.' Leslie shivered with a premonition of fear. 'But now they're out of liquor and getting restless. We sisters spent the whole day in church praying that something could be done before they did something drastic.'

'Well, that's what we're here for,' Murdock told Leslie, striking a heroic pose that was rendered absurd by his outfit.

Peck put aside his emotional quandary for the moment and concentrated on the more immediate concern of dealing with Salvador's men. A course of action fell into place and he told his partner, 'Murdock, you're going to have to get back to the others and let 'em know what's going on in here. I'll stay so at least one of us can be on the inside.'

'The others?' Leslie said. 'You brought the whole A-Team down here?'

Murdock and Peck looked at Leslie. Peck asked her, 'How'd you know about that?'

Leslie blushed and admitted, 'I've kept up with everything that's happened in your life... and I've prayed for you every night.'

'With some of the things we've pulled off,' Murdock said, 'I just knew someone had to be praying for us...'

TWENTY-SIX

Back in the mission's prime, the surrounding fields had been
cultivated by zealous parishioners into fertile vineyards that
had produced the finest wine-grapes to be found in the entire
region. Winemaking became a profitable sideline for the
missionaries, who used the increased income to pay for the
building of a larger church and adjacent schoolrooms, as
well as the tall adobe walls that came to surround the
courtyard. The mission had prospered, and for some time
the bishop had moved in at Santa Maria's and declared the
mission to be the new hub of his diocese. Then, in the course
of only a few years, the fortunes of the mission changed
dramatically. First a severe blight destroyed the vineyards,
ending the financial boom for the missionaries. The bishop
moved back to Cayambe, and many of the parishioners
drifted away from Santa Maria's in favour of the more
conveniently located church in nearby Catonya, where most
of them worked at the growing banana and coffee
plantations surrounding the small village. Santa Maria
steadily declined in significance, and at one point the mission
was abandoned for more than twenty years. It was only in
recent years that the establishment of the orphanage had
breathed new life into the desolate location. By then, wild
grass and weeds had obliterated nearly all traces of the
vineyards, and the only reminder of the mission's glory days
was the wine cellar, with its huge kegs and endless racks for
storing bottles. However, the kegs were empty now, as were
the bottles collecting dust in the racks. Gibbens, feeling the
first pangs of delirum tremens generating in his bones,
refused to believe that the cellar did not contain some

hidden, untapped supply of fine drink that had been left untouched these past decades. He individually inspected every one of the nearly two hundred bottles in the wine racks without stumbling upon so much as a drop to drink, then fell upon one of the kegs with a crowbar, determined to pry the lid open if that was what it would take to find something with which to quench his thirst.

'What kind of lousy wine cellar is this?!' he howeled miserably once the lid popped free and revealed that the inside of the keg was every bit as dry as the outer slats. 'Not one drop of bloody wine nowhere!'

Gibbens was a man of many voices, and when it became clear that he wasn't going to be able to get himself stinking drunk, his mind turned to other cravings. Thus, when he heard the shuffling of footsteps and saw the dim outlines of two nuns climbing down into the cellar, the unkempt Australian smacked his lips with anticipation and rubbed his palms together.

'Oh, now ain't this cute?' he sniggered once the two nuns had reached the bottom of the steps and realized Gibbens was standing before them. 'You two lovely ladies come all the way down here to keep ol' Gibbens company?'

Leslie stepped to one side and pointed up the stairs as she glared at Gibbens and demanded, 'You have no business down here! We've already told you there's no wine. Now would you kindly get out of here so we can be about our business?'

'And what business might that be?' Gibbens answered coyly, swaggering toward Leslie. 'Ah, you're the one I've had my eyes on all along, lassie. I think it's time you learned a few things that only a man can teach you . . .'

Gibbens hadn't been paying much attention to Murdock, and when he reached out to grab Leslie, he was suddenly interrupted by a tap on the shoulder.

'What about me, sailor?' Murdock cooed in a shrill falsetto, getting Gibbens to look his way. The Australian wasn't expecting much resistance from nuns, and he was totally unprepared for Murdock's sudden right cross. The gangly imposter's fist shot out of his sleeve like the blast from a cannon, and Gibbens reeled backwards with his arms flying wildly out on both sides. He was unconscious even before he finally keeled over and landed in a heap on the dirt floor. Murdock hurried over to make sure Gibbens was truly out cold, then made a quick Sign of the Cross and intoned, 'Do not pass "Go" and do not collect two hundred dollars.'

'What are you talking about?' Leslie asked Murdock.

'I know it's not the Lord's Prayer,' Murdock apologized, 'but it's the best I can do.'

Despite the gravity of their situation, Leslie couldn't help but grin at her ally. 'You're the one they call Howling Mad, aren't you?'

'What makes you say that?' Murdock asked innocently.

'Just a lucky guess.' Leslie went over to the large keg next to the one Gibbens had vandalized with the crowbar. She twisted the spigot a certain way, then felt underneath the framework supporting the keg until her fingers came in contact with a small lever. She pushed it and the top to the keg swung outward on a pair of unseen hinges, like a door. Murdock looked over Leslie's shoulder and saw that the keg was actually the entrance to a large tunnel leading from the cellar.

'How convenient,' Murdock remarked.

'We were told the tunnel was made many years ago, when there was persecution going on and the missionaries were helping to harbour fugitives. This leads to the grove outside the mission. Even if they're patrolling the courtyard walls they won't be able to see you come out.'

Murdock raised his hem and climbed into the opening. 'You sure you don't want to come with me?' he asked Leslie. 'You can be free and out of here in no time.'

'No,' Leslie responded firmly. 'They know my face too well. If I turned up missing during the head count, they'd take it out on the others. I can't let that happen. Go with God.'

'Hey, I always travel first class.' Murdock waved to Leslie, then headed off through the tunnel, which was carved out of the solid ground and large enough so that he only had to crouch slightly to avoid hitting his head against the ceiling.

As soon as Leslie closed the keg top behind him, the tunnel became immersed in darkness, but after Murdock had groped his way around the first bend, airshafts reaching down from the surface overhead also allowed light to filter into the passageway. The ground was layered with mud from the rain, and the air was as rich with the smell of mildew and decay as it was low on oxygen. Murdock began rationing breaths and picking up his pace, paying little heed to the mud that was splattering over his disguise.

At one point, the tunnel had collapsed in on itself, and Murdock was barely able to wriggle his way through a small opening to continue his escape. His lungs were beginning to burn and his head was feeling light from the shortage of oxygen. Fighting back his panic, Murdock pressed on, and finally came to a series of wooden steps built into a dirt incline, leading up to the surface. He leaned his weight against a thick oak door, and it gave way with a slow creak. As Leslie had told him, the tunnel opened out onto the grove of trees where the A-Team had first fled for cover when the *federales* had driven up to the mission.

'Hallelujah!' Murdock rejoiced, sucking in the fresh air as he stepped out into the open and stretched his cramped limbs. His celebration didn't last long, however, before he heard the snapping of a twig directly behind him. A rosary was the closest thing Murdock had to a weapon, and he clutched at the string of beads as if it were a bullwhip before he spun around to face whoever it was that had come up on him. His features lit up immediately and he gasped, 'Brother BA!'

'I ain't your brother, fool!' BA snarled.

Murdock was overcome with joy, though, and he flung himself through the air, ending up in BA's arms, looking like a liberalized nun who'd just married a Black Panther and was waiting to be carried across the threshhold of their new home. BA wanted no part of it, and he unceremoniously dumped Murdock to the ground as Hannibal and Amy joined them.

'Murdock, where's Face?' Hannibal asked.

Murdock stood up and adjusted his habit as he made a

petulant face at BA, then told Hannibal, 'He wanted to keep one man inside for protection. There's six mangy outlaws in there holding the sisters as hostages until their leader heals up.'

'Looks like we figured right,' Hannibal surmised. 'Is the leader's name Salvador?'

Murdock nodded.

Amy asked, 'Is Leslie all right?'

'She's holding on, but the guys are running out of booze, and it's making 'em nasty,' Murdock said. 'I had to floor one for getting fresh. I tell ya, Colonel, we gotta get in there real quick or there's going to be some very nasty business going down. Besides the nuns, there's gotta be twenty kids being held. That's a lot of targets for a handful of bad tempers.'

'Why can't we just get in the way you came out?' Amy inquried.

'Too risky. There's barely room going single file, and we'd be coming in blind,' Murdock explained. 'The tunnel leads to the wine cellar, and I get this feeling there's bound to be somebody there most of the time clawing around for more booze. We need a better plan.'

'I ain't dressing up as no nun!' BA declared adamantly.

Hannibal stared through the trees at the outline of the church. 'Well, it's a fairly simple maoeuvre, actually,' he said. 'All we have to do is get inside the mission without any of them knowing it, then clobber them. History must have recorded dozens of similar manoeuvres, right?'

'Name one,' BA challenged.

Murdock and Amy stared at Hannibal like game show emcees awaiting the answer to the day's big bonus quesiton.

'The Trojan Horse,' Hannibal finally said.

Amy turned to Murdock and shook her head, then told Hannibal, 'I think you better name another one.'

But Hannibal was already entertaining visions of a plan. 'It'll work,' he said confidently. 'It's just a question of getting the right horse...'

TWENTY-SEVEN

It was mid-afternoon when the A-Team returned to the ramshackle service station where they had bought gas and asked for directions at the start of their quest. The attendant was tending to his chickens again, this time crawling through the interior of an old Rambler for eggs. Surrounded by clucking hens, he didn't hear the chugging of the Bel-Air, and when Murdock suddenly peered in at him through the front windshield of the Rambler, the Ecuadorian shrieked with terror and dropped his basket of eggs.

'Hey hey, it's just me, my man!' Murdock said, then shifting into touristese, 'Pleeeese to be excusing, seeeeeñor, por favor.'

Once the attendant recognized Murdock, the fear left his face and he offered a relieved smile as he crawled out of the car, ignoring the splattered eggs that dripped down his legs. Amy was with Murdock, and she whispered, 'I'm sure glad he can take a yolk.'

'Amy, I'm surprised at you,' Murdock sniffed, 'making light of this man's misfortune like that.'

'What's the matter, Murdock, did I steal your line?' Amy replied. 'I think you're just jealous.'

The attendant was still a little nervous. He told Murdock and Amy, 'Banditos in Cayambe,' then pointed to the poster of Salvador he'd posted on the wall outside his office.

'You thought we were the bad guys?' Murdock asked.

The attendant nodded as he looked past Murdock at the Bel-Air, where the rest of the team was waiting. 'The Cheveeee, ees got no problems, no?'

'No, no problems,' Murdock said. 'We just want

159

sometheeng beeger.'

Amy was scanning the wrecks and she pointed to a decrepit delivery truck. 'How about that?'

The attendant stroked his chin as he shifted his gaze from the Chevy to the truck and back again. *'Este por esta?'*

'Si,' Murdock said. 'Even up, one for the other.'

After fiddling with his chin a few seconds longer, the native shrugged his shoulders and nodded.

'Ah, muchas gracias, muchaco,' Murdock said, patting the man on the back as he waved for the others to join them. BA first opened the trunk of the Chevy, then handed out several large canvas bags filled with a few selected items that had been removed from the jet before they had abandoned it outside Cayambe. Hannibal groaned from the weight of his load carrying it towards the truck.

Amy waited until the attendant had gone inside his office to clean his trousers, then said, 'He just traded away this truck for that broken-down Chevy. I can't believe it.'

'Well, this doesn't exactly look like something fresh off the assembly line,' Hannibal commented.

BA set down his load and got into the driver's seat of the truck. He turned the ignition, producing only a faint clicking sound under the hood. Glaring at Murdock, he shouted, 'At least the Chevy ran, man!'

'I think maybe he said something about it needing a little work,' Murdock offered lamely.

'BA, why don't you check under the hood while I go and have a talk with the manager here,' Hannibal said. 'We're gong to want to use a few stray parts around here, anyway. Murdock, before we give up the Chevy, why don't you try to track down a liquor store and buy a few cases of tequila or whatever's the cheapest booze you can get your hands on. Put it on Peck's tab. If you can find a load of empty boxes too, bring those. We will get this Trojan Horse put together yet!'

One of the canvas bags contained tools, and BA put them to work as soon as he'd raised the truck's hood and pinpointed the engine problems that needed correcting. Meanwhile, Amy opened the rear doors and started cleaning out the assorted trash cluttering the back. 'Compared to this, the work you did on that bread truck back in LA must seem like child's play,' she told BA.

'Don't remind me,' BA grumbled, scraping corrosion off the battery terminals. 'I just had to decorate that truck. This one I got to put back together from the inside out. I'm talkin' major surgery!'

Hannibal shortly returned from the office and told BA, 'We've got free run of the yard here. Any parts we need are ours. How's it look here?'

'Battery's shot. So's the starter and alternator,' BA said. 'Won't know how bad the engine is till we can turn the sucker over!'

'I saw another truck out back and looked like the same model, maybe a few years older,' Hannibal said. 'Between the two of 'em, we ought to be able to get something that'll make it as far as the mission before conking out. That's all we need.'

BA ventured off to salvage parts from the other truck while Hannibal helped Amy finish clearing out the interior of the main vehicle. Amy said, 'I don't know if this going to work, Hannibal. It's obvious that this truck's been sitting in a junkyard for years. Look at all this rust and flaking paint! I don't care how dark it might be when we get there, we're going to have trouble fooling anyone with this.'

'Sounds to me like you're going into the painting business, Amy,' Hannibal replied casually. 'I'm sure there's a bucket and brush around here somewhere. We don't need anything fancy, understand.'

Over the course of the next hour, the truck underwent a dramatic transformation. BA got the engine running, Amy slapped a thin coat of drab white paint over the rust spots and the rest of the exterior, and Murdock arrived with five cases of tequila and enough empty boxes to give the impression that the entire turck was filled with booze. Hannibal gingerly pried loose a few panels from other vehicles, and BA used a torch to weld them inside the hold of the truck, creating a false wall behind which four people could hide comfortably. Another hour was spent on fine touches, and by the time the sun was beginning to set behind the hills, the truck was loaded and ready to roll.

'Now, all I have to do is fuss in front of a mirror with my make-up kit,' Hannibal announced, 'Then we'll be ready for Troy!'

TWENTY-EIGHT

The visit to the mission by the *federales* that morning had given rise to increased paranoia amongst the renegades hiding out in the orphanage. Salvador was particularly wary, and before returning to his room after supper, he left orders for the courtyard and front gate to be guarded throughout the night by his men. None of the others were willing to volunteer for the task, and so it was decided to play a few quick rounds of poker as the sun set, with the understanding that whoever had lost the most money by the time the sun had sunk from view would also be responsible for keeping the night watch. Swain, the American, had proposed the poker-playing, figuring his gambling experience would earn him a tidy profit as well as a daily reprieve from having to do guard duty. Lady Luck turned her back on him, however, and that first night it was Swain who was sent out to pace the courtyard until dawn.

Without liquor to liven up the evenings, the others followed Salvador's cue and turned in earlier than normal after assuring the Mother Superior that they were all light sleepers and would certainly be awakened by any attempts on the part of the nuns or chilren to escape from the orphanage. Swain figured that no one was about to double-check if he was performing his duties, and after he had circled the courtyard interior several times, he crawled off into an alcove hear the main gate and sprawled out on the bench there. Holding his automatic rifle across his lap, he tucked in his chin and slumped over slightly, making himself as comfortable as possible. Within minutes, he was drifting off to sleep. Before he could fully submerge himself into the realm of dreams, however, someone outside the main gate pulled a bell rope and the large brass bell above Swain's head clanged loudly. Swain sprang upright like a punchdrunk boxer who'd just been given a whiff of smelling salts. Rushing to the orphanage, he ran into the Mother Superior, who had already heard the clamour and was coming out.

'Good goin', lady,' Swain said as he escorted the nun back to the gate, his rifle in his hand. 'I don't have to tell you what to do, do I?'

The Mother Superior shook her head as she reached the gate and raised the bolt across it. Swain stayed behind her, out of sight, as she slowly creaked the gate open and peered out. A middle-aged man with dark, straggly hair and a beat-up hat stood before her. When he saw that he was addressing a nun, he pulled off his hat and wrung it in his hands.

"Scuse me, Sister,' he mumbled demurely, 'I hate t' bother yer... I know it's late... but, my truck... it broke down a little way from here.' The man gestured over his shoulder at the vehicle parked on the shoulder of the road a dozen yards away.

The Mother Superior thought there was something familiar about the man's voice and appearance, but she didn't associate either one of them with one of the men who had spoken to her about Leslie Becktall that morning. Shaking her head, she apologized, 'I'm sorry, but there's nothing we can do for you.'

Hannibal could feel his false moustache peeling loose from his upper lip, and he quickly pressed it back into place as he stepped forward and prevented the nun from closing the gate on him. He pleaded, raising his voice slightly, 'But, Sister, I have to deliver the whiskey. If I don't deliver the whiskey, my boss will –'

There was a sudden interruption as Swain pulled the nun away from the opening in the gateway and took her place. He eyed Hannibal over, then demanded, 'Where'd you say this truckload of whiskey was?'

'Over there, señor,' Hannibal said, pointing to the refurbished truck. 'If I could just have someone –'

'Don't you worry, pal,' Swain told him. 'You've come to

the right place. We missionary tupes are real helpful to our fellow man... ain't that right, sister?'

The Mother Superior nodded weakly, but her expression clearly contradicted the gesture. Turning her back on Hannibal, she headed back to the orphanage.

'Bless yer,' Hannibal said, smiling gratefully at Swain.

'My pleasure, ace, I assure you.' Swain turned around and cupped his hands over his mouth as he shouted, 'Gibbens, haul that Aussie rear o' yers out here, on the double!'

As they were waiting for the Australian, Hannibal coughed lightly into his fist, then said, 'I think it's my starter. If you just have a flashlight, I could take –'

'Don't worry, friend, we'll take care of you... you say it's whiskey you're carryin'? Much of it?'

'Actually, it's mostly tequila. A few cases...'

Gibbens finally staggered out into the courtyard, rubbing the back of his neck. 'What the hell you want?' he asked Swain. 'You won the job fair and square, so don't –'

'Put a lid on it and listen,' Swain cut in, barely able to restrain his excitement. Gesturing at Hannibal, he explained, 'This here's a man whose whiskey truck just broke down right outside these walls. He wonders if we might be able to help him out.'

Gibbens glanced over Hannibal's shoulder at the truck, and a smile widened across his face as he began to chuckle lightly. Swain joined in the disquieting laughter. Hannibal pretended to be unaware of the reason for their mirth and only smiled in apparent confusion. Gibbens rushed back into the orphanage, and returned moments later with Marcos, Sanchez, and Bantu behind him, all dressing quickly as they ran.

'We'll fix you up right proper,' Gibbens promised Hannibal as he pulled the main gates open all the way. 'You just stay put and leave everything to us. We're Good Samaritans, we are. Right, boys?'

'You got it!' Swain howled as he rushed out to the truck and climbed up into the cabin. As he shifted the truck into neutral, the others leaned their combined weight against the back end and slowly pushed the vehicle into the courtyard, cheering themselves on noisily. The commotion roused the other nuns, and a few of them came outside to see what was going on, including Leslie and Face, who was back to wearing his disguise.

'What's going on, Templeton?' Leslie asked.

Peck looked over at Hannibal, seeing through his partner's masquerade instantly. 'I'm not sure,' Peck told Leslie, 'but I got a feeling it's part of some master plan.'

Once the truck was in the middle of the courtyard, Bantu and Marcos closed the gates and Gibbens yanked the rear doors open. His eyes lit up like those of a child on Christmas morning when he saw the stacked boxes filling the truck's hold. He ripped open the cover of the box closest to him and pulled out a bottle of tequila.

'Bingo!' he screamed in exultation. 'It's party time, mates!'

'W... w... wait!' Hannibal stammered timidly as he shuffled over towards the truck. 'Watcher doin' with my whiskey?'

'We're lightening your load, my friend,' Swain told Hannibal. 'I'll bet the ol' truck'll run much better without all this weight holdin' it down.'

'But...' Hannibal watched helplessly as the men formed a human chain and passed out all of the boxes in the back of the truck, including the ones that had been filled with car parts and sealed tightly to give the impression they contained more booze. Once the truck had been emptied, several bottles were passed around and the men swilled the tequila greedily, spilling as much as they swallowed. Swain closed the truck doors and gave Hannibal a sharp part on the back.

'Hey, it's not your booze, pal, is it?' he said. 'You couldn't help it if you were robbed at gunpoint a few miles north of here, could you? Right? You follow me, gramps?'

As Hannibal was playing along with the renegades, inside the truck's hold Murdock and BA carefully removed aside the false wall they and Amy had been crouched behind. Giving themselves more room to move, the trio stretched out and Murdock ignited a match so they could see each other.

'The Trojan Horse has arrived,' Murdock whispered.

'Yeah,' BA muttered. 'Now all we gotta do is sit on our

butts in the dark till they all get drunk!'

'From the sound out there, I don't think it'll be too long,' Amy said hopefully.

Outside, the renegades were content enough for the time being with the tequila in the one box they'd opened. Each of the men had his own bottle, and there was no reason to bother with inspecting the other boxes. After taking a long draw off his bottle, Gibbens sauntered over to the orphanage doorway, where Leslie was standing with Sister Peck. The liquor was already fuelling the Australian's baser instincts, and he leered contemptuously at Leslie. 'There's a little something I owe you for that swing ya took at me earlier,' he told Leslie. 'What say we find a room to ourselves to discuss it, eh?'

Before Gibbens could grab Leslie, Hannibal came up from behind and clamped a firm hand on the Australian's shoulder, complaining, 'See here, I don't think it's right, what yer doin' with my whiskey...'

'It's not whiskey, you oaf, it's tequila!' Gibbens railed, spinning around and grabbing Hannibal by the throat. Hannibal didn't put up much of a fight as the outlaw from the outback poured some of the liquor down his throat, shouting, 'There, can't you tell the difference?'

While Hannibal went into gagging convulsions to distract Gibbens, Peck whisked Leslie back into the orphanage. Hannibal dropped to his knees and held onto his sides as if he were in misery. 'Ohhhhhh,' he groaned.

'There now,' Gibbens taunted, 'don't that make things a lot better? Relax and enjoy yourself, all right? The night's young...'

TWENTY-NINE

The night may have started out young, but it aged quickly. Overjoyed at the unanticipated arrival of so much tequila, the renegades celebrated by starting a massive bonfire in the centre of the courtyard and gathering around it to sing bawdy songs and swap tall tales about their various misadventures prior to the time when they had all banded together under Salvador's leadership. Whenever the fire began to dim, a couple of the men would stagger inside for a few more scraps of broken furniture to offer in sacrifice to the flickering blaze. Because the men were no strangers to long bouts of drinking, their steady intake of tequila didn't achieve the results Hannibal had intended. As the hours dragged on, none of the outlaws showed any signs of losing consciousness. If anything, the liquor seemed to make the men more lively, jerking them from the doldrums they'd been in all day.

Hannibal sat off to one side, brooding in the shadows as he pretended to nurse a bottle of tequila. He was sober, though, struggling to remain patient and waiting for the best opportunity to initiate the follow-up to Operation Trojan Horse. At one point, shortly after midnight, Peck slipped out of the orphanage and came to Hannibal's side.

'I say we should go for it, Hannibal!'

'No way,' Hannibal muttered. 'Look at 'em. They're all toting their guns, and even if they're drunk, they'd still be able to cause problems before I could get the others out of the truck.'

'We could create some kind of diversion inside the orphanage,' Peck suggested.

Hannibal shook his head again. 'I'd just as soon keep them away from the women and children when they're this drunk. Who knows what they'd stoop to if they felt provoked? No, Face, we're just gonna have to wait and stick to the game plan. I think you should stay inside and make sure everybody else does, too. You'll be able to hear it when you're needed.'

Peck sighed and adjusted the headpiece of his habit, then headed back to the orphanage. Hannibal stayed put and waited. And waited.

At a little after four in the morning, Marcos and Sanchez yawned and stumbled away from the fire before passing out on the ground. That left Gibbens, Swain, and Bantu, who all continued singing for almost another hour. Then, while Gibbens went to get more firewood, Bantu began babbling in his native tongue, and by the time Gibbens returned with an armload of broken desks, the African's monologue had put Swain to sleep.

'Shut up, Bantu!' Gibbens snapped as he fed the fire. 'Nobody wants to hear your gibberish!'

Bantu was offended by the insult, and he leaped to his feet. The sudden movement was more than his equilibrium could stand, however, and before he could raise a fist in anger at Gibbens, he blacked out and crumpled to the ground next to Swain. His rifle fell into the fire, and Gibben had to kick it away before the heat exploded any of the bullets housed in the weapon's ammo clip.

'Bloody upstart!' Gibbens mumbled to himself as he sat down before the fire and picked up his bottle. He had a clear view of Hannibal and called out to him, 'Hey, you! Come have a drink with me!'

Hannibal's head was turned down, and he pretended to be asleep. Gibbens called out to him again, then gave up and consoled himself with a few more drinks. By now the grey tinge of dawn was creeping into the air. Gibbens stared at the fire until it died, then finished his bottle and flung it into the glowing embers.

'I want more!' he howled, rising to his feet and moving uncertainly over to the stacked boxes near the truck. The

169

moment he turned his back to Hannibal in order to pry open one of the boxes, Hannibal gingerly climbed to his feet and slipped across the ground to the rear doors. He had his hands on the handle at the same moment that Gibbens discovered that the box he'd opened contained an old muffler instead of more tequila. 'What the bloody hell! I don't want this! I want more booze, damn it!'

Throwing open the truck doors, Hannibal shouted, 'You hear that, BA? The man says he needs a good shot of something. How about helping the poor guy out?'

There was a loud crashing sound as BA shoved the makeshift wall out of the truck and then jumped down to the ground, followed by Murdock and Amy. Gibbens stared with disbelief at the force that had so suddenly materialized before his eyes.

'Swain! Bantu!' he shouted. 'Marcos! Sanchez! Get yer drunken butts awake! We got company!'

Gibbens had neglected to carry his gun over to the boxes, and Hannibal was able to overtake him before he could backtrack to the fire to rearm himself. The Australian launched a roundhouse punch, but Hannibal ducked it easily and tackled Gibbens. The two men crashed into the boxes, overturning them. Loose auto parts spilled free, and Gibbens got his hands on a tire iron with which to defend himself. Hannibal countered by plucking up the old muffler pipe, and the two foes engaged in a bout of savage fencing.

Meanwhile, Amy and Murdock outraced the two Cuban brothers to their weapons and forced Marcos and Sanchex to stand spread-eagled against the side of the truck. BA and Bantu fell on one another like heavyweight wrestling champions and tumbled across the ground, trading blows. BA had the advantage in that he wasn't drunk, and when his foe's strength quickly sapped away, the skirmish between them ended with Bantu groaning in misery.

Peck led the contingent of nuns out onto the front porch of the orphanage to watch the last few blows traded between Hannibal and Gibbens. The Australian managed to snap Hannibal's muffler pipe in half, but he couldn't keep up with Hannibal's footwork. Borrowing a page from the 'Muham-

170

med Ali Book of Sparring', Hannibal played rope-a-dope and wore Gibbens down with his artful dodges and retreats. Finally Gibbens dropped his guard one second too long, and Hannibal lashed out with a karate kick that caught the Australian in the midsection and bowled him over. Murdock tossed Hannibal a gun, and the battle was officially over. As if to celebrate the occasion, the sun began to rise in the east.

'Okay, pal,' Hannibal said between breaths as he prodded Gibbens to his feet. 'Into the back of the truck, along with the rest of your playmates!'

While the drunken renegades were being herded into the truck, Peck headed back inside the orphanage, already starting to change out of his nun's habit like Clark Kent hustling to change into Superman. By the time Murdock was getting ready to close the rear doors of the truck on the prisoners, Peck emerged with Salvador slung over his shoulder. The ringleader swore and kicked, but he was too weak to break loose from Peck's humiliating hold.

'Hold on, Murdock!' Hannibal said, 'Looks like we got one more.'

'You will pay for this!' Salvador warned Peck before he was tossed into the back of the truck.

'I know I will,' Peck retorted. 'I got friends keeping tack of my tab for me. Putting a slime like you away will make it all worth it, though, I promise you!'

As the A-Team was piling into the front of the truck, the Mother Superior elbowed her way through the other nuns and rushed forward to confront Hannibal. 'Who are you people?' she wanted to know. 'What are you doing?'

'Mornin', Sister,' Hannibal said graciously. 'We just stopped by to help you take out the trash. I hope you don't mind.' He climbed up onto the back bumper and thumped his fist on the side of the truck. BA started up the engine with no problem and started pulling out of the courtyard. Hannibal waved at the nuns and called out, 'We'll be back in a little bit to help you clean this mess up.'

THIRTY

The truck sputtered and protested every inch of the way, but BA managed to drive it up into the highlands, past a sprinkling of homes and small farm plots to a wide, sprawling tract of open countryside. By now the sun was high overhead, hardening tracks in the muddy road and burning off the morning dew that clung to the wild grasses. Hannibal was still riding along on the back bumper, and he leaned out to one side so that BA could see him wave in the rear-view mirror.

'I think this is far enough!' Hannibal called out. 'Let's give this truck a breather!'

'I'll stop, but I ain't turnin' off the engine,' BA shouted over his shoulder. 'No tellin' if it'd start up again!'

Once the truck had rolled to a halt, Hannibal jumped down to the ground and took a few steps back, levelling his rifle at the rear doors as Murdock and Peck came back to open them.

'Everybody out!' Peck told the renegades, cocking the hammer on his pistol for emphasis.

The prisoners sullenly crawled out of the vehicle, grimacing under the glaring rays of the sun. Bruised and hung over, they didn't pose much of a threat to the A-Team at the moment. When Salvador paused weakly at the edge of the truck's hold, summoning the strength to climb down to the ground, Swain and Gibbens came over to help. He spat at them and drove them away with a lacklustre swat from his hand as he raged, 'You stinking, drunken slobs! This is your fault! How could you be so stupid!'

The others looked away in shame as Salvador lowered

himself to the ground and stood with wavering pride on his own. Although he was still ailing, he seemed to have gained a little more strength during the night. Then again, it might have been his bristling anger that helped prop him up.

'This is it, fellas,' Hannibal told Salvador and his men. 'The party's over. And just to let you know how much we enjoyed your company, we want you to leave us with some souvenirs. I want you all stripped down to your underwear. Now!'

'This some kinda joke?' Swain exclaimed.

Hannibal lowered his rifle and sent a few bursts digging into the mud near Swain's feet. 'If I'm joking, those are my punchlines, and I got plenty more of 'em. Now I said strip!'

While the bandits warily undressed, BA pulled off the road and turned the truck around so that it was pointed back in the direction of the mission. Murdock and Peck moved in and gathered up the prisoners' clothes, removing contents from the pockets.

'Well, well, well,' Peck said as he began coming across large wads of currency and bits of expensive jewellery tucked away in the men's clothing. 'Looks like you boys had been busy before you went into hiding, eh? I guess I owe you a bit of thanks, because I figure there's enough here to subsidize our whole trip down here and back. How about that, Hannibal?'

'To the victor goes the spoils,' Hannibal said. To the prisoners, he added, 'What can I say, guys? Easy come, easy go.'

'Have your jokes while you can, gringos,' Salvador advised the A-Team. 'The last laugh will be ours.'

'Maybe so, but we won't be around to hear it.' Hannibal closed the doors and climbed back up on the bumper while Murdock and Peck got back in the front of the truck. As BA started back downhill, Hannibal gave Salvador and his men a mock salute and cried out jovially, 'Happy tanning, boys! I think if you head the other way, you might reach the border by sundown. I hear they have openings for exotic dancers at the Colombian Kit Kat Klub. You're already dressed for the occasion; all you have to do is practise your moves!'

The underdressed thugs hurled curses at Hannibal as the truck headed away from them, then turned their anger on one another, trading blame for the lack of vigilance that had led to their undoing.

Lighting up a fresh cigar, Hannibal started climbing up to the roof of the truck so that he could stretch out for the ride back to the mission. Before he could reach his destination, however, he heard a sickly sound from the engine up front, followed by a sudden and disturbing silence. The truck continued to roll downhill, but it was gravity rather than horsepower that was responsible for the movement.

'What happened!?' Hannibal shouted.

'The engine gave out, that's what happened,' BA shouted back. As the truck picked up speed and began bounding harshly over the hardened ruts in the road, BA added, with a trace of anxiety, 'So did the brakes!'

'How charming,' Hannibal muttered, bracing himself. 'And to think I didn't bring along my AA membership card for emergency road service.'

Fortunately, the truck's steering was still operational, and BA was able to keep the vehicle on the road, taking corners wide and trying to veer back and forth on the straight sections in the hope of slowing down their momentum.

'The parking brake!' Amy shouted, leaning forward between Murdock and Peck in the front sea. 'BA, try the parking brake!'

'I already did, and there ain't one!' BA told her. 'There ain't no drag chute, either. We're in trouble!'

There were several times when the truck nearly overturned from the force with which it rounded corners, and once MA avoided a head-on collision with a farm tractor by mere inches when the other vehicle rolled into an intersection a quarter-mile from the mission. At last, however, they were out of the hills and the road levelled off, allowing the truck to slow down. As the mission came into view, BA tightened his grip on the steering wheel, and cried out, 'Hold on, 'cause I'm goin' through the field to slow us down some more!'

Hannibal clung to the back of the truck while the others braced themselves in front and BA left the road, ploughing into the waist-high grass surrounding the mission. As he'd hoped, the density of the grass and the softness of the damp soil below it combined to ease the truck's headlong flight, and by the time he'd steered the vehicle through the main gate and into the courtyard, they were travelling at less than five miles an hour. BA swerved to avoid a trio of nuns standing out in the open, at the same time crashing into the stacked boxes that had been unloaded from the truck the night before. The collision succeeded in bringing the truck to a stop a few yards shy of the front entrance to the orphanage. The passengers were shaken up from the ordeal, but no one was injured.

'Whew!' Murdock said, taking a deep breath. Turning to BA, he cracked, 'All I gotta say is you gotta lotta nerve complaining about my flying, BA!'

'Shut up, fool!' BA said. 'I drive like this when I gotta. You fly like a maniac 'cause you like to! There's a big difference!'

'Okay, knock it off, you two,' Peck said as he opened his door and climbed out of the truck. 'We're back in one piece, that's what matters.'

As Hannibal jumped to the ground and circled around to join Peck, the Mother Superior strode over to them, indignation written all over her face. 'This is a terrible thing you have done!' she accused.

'Well, I'm sorry, Sister,' Hannibal apologized, 'but we had a few problems with the truck and the best we could manage was a crash-landing.'

'I'm not talking about that. I mean what you did with those men. You might have meant well, but it was a stupid thing to do.'

Hannibal looked at Peck as if he couldn't believe what he'd just heard. 'Stupid? Did she say stupid?'

'Yes, stupid,' the nun repeated.

Hannibal shook some loose ash from his cigar, then stared hard at the Mother Superior. 'Lady, we just got rid of a bunch of slobs who have been driving you nuts for the past couple of weeks. Now we didn't expect a reward from you – a simple 'thank you', maybe – but we *didn't* expect you to call us stupid.'

'I assure you,' the nun retorted, 'a "thank you" would have been forthcoming, if you had got rid of them. But all you did was humiliate them and make them want revenge. And they will return for it. I know it.'

'So we'll get rid of them again,' Peck said. 'They're only six marginally competent outlaws. And they don't even have weapons.'

Murdock added, 'Right now they don't even have clothes.'

'But they have friends,' the Mother Superior declared.

This took Hannibal by surprise. 'Friends?' He looked at Peck and Murdock. 'You guys were the inside men. How come no one mentioned that they had friends?'

'This is the first I've heard of it,' Peck said.

The elder nun said, 'I overheard them talking the past few nights about meeting up with their reinforcements. That's why I was trying to keep all of this as low-key as possible, hoping their associates wouldn't find them. Now you've probably delivered them to their allies.'

'How many?' Hannibal said, a sinking feeling in his stomach. 'How many men are they supposed to be linking up with?'

The Mother Superior said nothing, but the look of worry in her face spoke volumes.

'That many, huh?' Peck said bleakly.

THIRTY-ONE

Over a hasty breakfast, the A-Team plotted their next course of action. It was decided that they had no choice but to assume that Salvador would return with his reinforcements to seek vengeance against anyone they might be able to get their hands on in the mission. Likewise, everyone knew that there was no way they were going to leave the nuns and chilren to fend for themselves against the avengers.

'Our Trojan Horse scheme was a great offence,' Hannibal summed it up, 'but now we have to start thinking in terms of defence. It's a whole new ball game.'

As the A-Team quickly toured the mission, they took an inventory of everything and anything that could possibly be used as a weapon and brainstormed constantly to redefine and finetune their strategy, taking into consideration the additional materials. Finally it was time to dispense with planning and begin carrying out the actual preparations for battle. After taking a quick crash course from BA, Amy began accumulating an arsenal of handmade molotov cocktails, manufactured by mixing gasoline and other inflammable liquids into empty wine bottles and stuffing the tops with rags. Murdock stopped by to inspect one of Amy's first attempts at the crude bombs, picking up the bottle and sniffing the gaseous vapours rising through the rag plug.

'Hmmmmm, a good year, to be sure,' Murdock sniffed with aristocratic panache, 'but the bouquet leaves a lot to be desired. Inferior body, as well, I must say...'

'It may not taste good, but I bet it'll knock you off your feet if you let it,' Amy joked back. 'You better keep that bottle away from Hannibal while he's smoking, too.'

Murdock was carrying a load of lumber under one arm, and he brought it over a corner of the courtyard where Face and Leslie were doing some carpentry work. Specifically, Leslie was holding guns in place while Peck attached them to two-by-fours, which in turn were connected to a long beam.

'I got some more two-by-fours and half-a-dozen wood dowels,' Murdock said, setting down his load. 'I hope they'll do the trick.'

'Let's find out.' Peck raised the large beam and set a pair of the dowels underneath it. When he set down the beam, it rolled back and forth on the dowels with little resistance. 'Yeah, these'll be fine, Murdock. Good job.'

Murdock stood by a few seconds, then realized that Peck and Leslie were waiting for him to leave. 'Well, no time to stand idle, troops,' he said, backing away. 'I guess I'll go see how my ol' buddy BA's doing...'

'You do that,' Peck told him.

BA was sorting through the boxes filled with auto parts, testing the strengths of various used shock absorbers. He'd already removed the shocks from the delivery truck and affixed them to long slats of wood taken from the church pews. A group of orphans were following him around as he worked, gaping in awe at what he was doing.

'BA, ol' buddy!' Murdock called out as he swaggered over. 'How's thing's comin' on your end?'

'How's it *look* like I'm comin', fool?!' BA answered testily. 'This is tough work! I always get stuck doin' the tough work!'

'That's because you're the toughest we got,' Murdock said. 'You should feel honoured.'

'Ha!' BA shook his head with disgust, then managed a smile for his youthful admirers. 'These kids are cool, man! They wouldn't make me fly when I don't wanna, and they wouldn't call me a bad driver when I save 'em from gettin' hurt in a runaway truck, either!'

'Oh, still sore about that, are you?' Murdock said. 'I already told you I was sorry.'

'Forget it!' BA pointed over at the fake wall they'd used inside the truck for the Trojan Horse scheme. 'Go take that thing over to Hannibal. He says he needs it, and I don't got

178

time to lug it over to him if I'm gonna get these suckers made on time.'

Jutting his lower lip out, Murdock walked over to the sheet of metal propped against the side of the truck. Before picking it up, he reached into his pocket and pulled out his pet golfball. 'I tell ya, GB, you think it's bad being a golfball, try being a gofer sometime. It's not pretty, GB, not pretty at all.'

The sheet was so wide across that Murdock could barely secure a firm enough grip on it to carry it. He veered awkwardly under the piece, forced to walk sideways so he could see where he was going. Several of the children watched him and began laughing as they broke away from BA to follow him. By the time he reached the porch, where Hannibal was pounding a wooden truss onto the frame of a swivel office chair, Murdock was perspiring heavily and breating in deep, laboured gulps.

'Why'd you bring that over all by yourself, Murdock?' Hannibal asked him as he came over to help transfer the metal sheet onto the truss.

'We all have our cross to bear, as the good Sister would say,' Murdock intoned. 'I bear mine without complaint.'

'I'm impressed,' Hannibal said, leaning on the chair to counterblanace the added weight of the metal sheet. 'Let me see if I can't come up with a medal for you when this is all over. In the meantime, help me shift the weight around on this chair so I'll be able to sit in it without falling over.'

Hannibal and Murdock shifted the truss and the sheet around until they served their purpose of providing a movable shield behind which Hannibal could sit in the swivel chair and fire a gun through small slits in the sheeting. As Hannibal was testing the manoeuvrability of the contraption, the Mother Superior stepped out into the courtyard for the first time since breakfast and let out a shriek of horror.

'Oh oh,' Murdock said, watching the nun storm towards him and Hannibal. 'I think it must have been the pews...'

But the Mother Superior was upset about more than the use of church pews in the defence of the mission. 'I will not stand for this!' she said, taking in the whole range of munitions the A-Team had put together while she was napping. 'I have innocent children to protect. What are you planning to do with all these guns and everything else you're putting together?'

'We plan to shoot at the bad guys when they show their ugly faces,' Hannibal replied casually. 'That's how this kind of plan works, Sister. I hope you didn't think we were going to fill squirt guns with Holy Water and try to scare 'em off that way...'

'Spare me your blasphemy,' the nun retorted indignantly. 'I will not allow gunfire in the courtyard area. It's too risky.'

'You and the other Sisters are going to hide in the wine cellar with the children once things start happening,' Hannibal told her. 'As for us, we need the guns and whatever else we can use in case they get through the gate... unless you've got some miracles up your sleeves you'd like to share with me.'

There was a standoff between Hannibal and the Mother Superior that lasted for several seconds, with neither side talking, but there was a clash of wills nonetheless. Before either party could back down or escalate their differences, Peck and Leslie came by, carrying the mobile gun rack.

'Colonel,' Peck said, 'This thing's about ready to use, but I just found out that we aren't gonna be able to mount it where we wanted to because of the roof.'

'What's wrong with the roof?' Hannibal asked.

'There's a few leaks in it,' Leslie explained. 'We were in the midst of fixing it when Salvador and his men showed up. They wouldn't let us finish, because they were afraid we'd try to signal for help from the roof while we were up there.'

Hannibal took a few steps back and rose on his tip-toes to get a better view of the roof. 'Were you by any chance using tar to fix the leaks?'

'Why, yes,' Leslie said. 'We had enough donated to us to do the whole roof, and it's just been sitting in one of the back storage rooms since those men came.'

'Why do you ask?' the Mother Superior asked suspiciously. 'You aren't planning to make some sort of bomb out of tar, are you?'

'Not exactly,' Hannibal said as he scanned the courtyard area in front of the main gates. 'Sister, do you follow baseball much?'

'I beg your pardon?'

'Baseball. Do you know what a relief pitcher is?'

'No, not really.'

'Well, a relief pitcher is sort of like Plan B; something you can fall back on if at first you don't succeed.'

The Mother Superior frowned, becoming more confused by the moment. 'What does any of that have to do with the tar?'

'Everything,' Hannibal said, his eyes twinkling. 'I think maybe I've found a way to solve a few of our problems here. Murdock, Peck, go with Leslie and track down that tar. If you find some shovels, bring those with you, too. We've got a lot of digging to do.'

'We're not going to dig another tunnel, are we, Colonel?' Murdock asked.

Hannibal shook his head. 'No, Murdock, I was thinking more along the lines of a major breakthrough in trench warfare.'

The Mother Superior made a face and turned her back to Hannibal as she started for the church. 'I'm going to pray.'

'That's not a bad idea,' Hannibal called out to her. 'While you're at it, make sure you say a few for us. We're going to need 'em...'

THIRTY-TWO

The criminal reinforcements the Mother Superior had overheard Salvador talking about were twelve men who made the Dirty Dozen look like a Boy Scout troop. They shared Salvador's Cuban roots and, more than a month ago, they had set out from Havana after receiving word from Salvador that he'd grown weary of small-scale crime and wanted to put together a small army with which he could overthrow one of the smaller Caribbean islands and become an international power broker. The plan was for the Cubans to meet Salvador's Ecuadorian gang in the hills outside Cayambe, where they would drill and then try their hand at insurrection with some local villages before heading back north to the Caribbean. Unaware that their leader had been injured in a shootout shortly after wiring for them to come south, the reinforcements had taken the scenic route to South America, pausing to terrorize no fewer than ten Caribbean islands on the way to bolster a war chest. Their speciality had been sniffing out the biggest dope dealers in any given port, then ripping them off for their stash and cash before heading out to sea and another island where they could repeat the same tactics. By the time they had reached the mainland in Venezuela, the twelve men had amassed a fortune too tempting to last all the way to Ecuador. Some of the plunder was spent on a binge of high living and gambling, some was used to pay off a few border patrol officers threatening to make trouble, and still more was lost when they spent a night in the Colombian capitol of Bogata and were victimized by a gang of street children who burgled their rooms while they were whoring at a local brothel. By the time they'd crossed the border into Ecuador, the Cubans were broke, destitute, and in bad need of leadership. Twenty-seven miles outside Cayambe, they had ambushed a transport truck carrying green bananas to the nearet distribution centre. They still had the truck, along with the dozen stomach aches that came from eating too many green bananas, when fate had seen fit to reunite them with their ailing leader and his underdressed cohorts that afternoon. After raiding a farmhouse for clothing, food, and antacid, the revitalized forces of Salvador set their sights on the Santa Maria mission. Salvador assured his newly-arrived comrades that the mission would indeed be a nice place for them to take out their frustrations and to practise the bttling techniques by which they would later conquer their very own island kingdom.

It was shortly before dusk when they arrived outside the mission. The place seemed barren and deserted, but Salvador knew better. Leaning out the passenger's window in the truck, he summoned his strength and shouted, 'Hey! Your lovely holiness! We have come back to crush the dogs who dared to humiliate us this morning! I know they are there, I can smell them! You be good Sisters and give us what we want . . . then maybe we go away. If not . . . then maybe we burn your church to the ground and show you just how mad we can be!'

There was no response from inside the mission. Salvador carefully climbed out of the truck, then leaned against the front fender as he motioned for half his force to begin circling around the large walls of the courtyard in the hope of sneaking in through the back entrance used by the priest during his bi-weekly visits. The rest of the men took up positions around the main entrance and waited with Sanchez for an answer from within.

'We give you one more chance, Sisters. Send out your friends and no harm will come to you, I promise!' As he spoke, Salvador was cocking the pistol he'd taken from one of the reinforcements. He counted off ten seconds, then fired six consecutive shots into the thick wood of the main gate.

'We mean business!' Swain shouted next to Salvador

when the gunshots failed to produce results. He was ready to
fire off a full round of ammunition from his automatic rifle
when two objects suddenly came hurtling over the courtyard
fence at them. They were Molotov cocktails, and while they
fell wide of their mark and only one of them actually
exploded, the declaration of war had been officially
proclaimed.

The battle was on.

At the rear of the mission, Hannibal Smith was perched
on the rectory rooftop in his customized swivel chair.
Peering through the slats in his protective shield, he waited
until he could see the whites of the Cuban's eyes, then
squeezed off a round from his machine gun, taking gouges
out of the adobe where the men were trying to scale the walls.
Not wishing to lose their fingers, the attackers let go and fell
back to the ground, turned back from their first offensive.

Back in front, Swain emptied his gun into the middle of
the main gates in an obvious effort to weaken the wooden
bolt holding them shut. Bantu and Marcos were rushing
forward with a makeshift battering ram when another
Molotov cocktail spun over the walls toward them. They
dived to the ground as the bottle exploded, turning the log
they'd been carrying into kindling.

Sanchez and three other men tried the right wall adjacent
to the church. He managed to lasso a weather-vane that was
sturdy enough to support his weight, then pulled himself up
the sides of the wall. Reaching the top, he peered into the
courtyard and saw Amy lighting another firebomb near the
main entrance. After checking around to make sure no one
had seen him, Sanchez climbed over the top of the wall and
crouched on a length of scaffolding while he signalled for the
other two men to silently follow him up. From his
perspective, the Cuban wasn't able to see that the scaffolding
was being supported by a set of rigged shock absorbers that
in turn were connected to a hydraulic pump being operated
by BA from the concealment of the mission's trash
dumpster. Once all three of the would-be infiltrators were
standing on the scaffolding at the same time, BA triggered
the pump. With an incredible jolt, the scaffolding sprang

upward at a sharp angle, like a wide diving board that someone had just jumped on with all their might. With screams of shock, Sanchez and his men were catapulted back over the wall, arms flailing wildly until the hard ground ended their falls.

Face was operating a similar booby trap near the opposite wall, and he managed to turn back another group of men trying to climb into the courtyard. Meanwhile, Murdock was manipulating the broad beam with the mounted guns, rolling the beam back and forth as he pulled a set of taut wires connected to the guns' triggers, setting off simultaneous discharges that gave the impression that a full firing squad was doing sniper duty on the rooftop of the orphanage. Because each member of the A-Team had stocked up on ammunition from the large cache they had found during their inventory of the mission, it was possible for them to continually repulse the repeated attempts by Salvador's men to gain entry to the mission. Bullets flew in both directions without relief, and the air echoed with the din of gunfire and the aftershocks of home-made bombs. All the while the sun came closer to setting, threatening to throw the whole conflict into a new perspective.

Salvador's frustration mounted as he saw more and more of his men returning to the truck, having failed to get inside the mission compound. Remaining crouched behind the front fender, he kept firing at the main gates in the vain hope that persistence would win him the day. Marcos finally ran to his side to deliver the news he knew too well already.

'No one has made it over the wall, Salvador! They have been joined by reinforcements, too, I am sure of it!'

'Pah!' Salvador spat in the dirt. 'More likely it is mere nuns with guns that keep you cowering like frightened children at the base of the walls!'

'Not so!' Marcos protested. 'We have scaled the walls several times, only to be hurled back! We have tried everything!'

'Not everything!' Salvador saw an unexploded Molotov cocktail land in the soft grass a few yards away from the truck. With reckless desperation, he pushed himself away from the fender and dived for the bottle, grabbing it and throwing it back toward the mission before it exploded. His aim had been good, and the firebomb went off against the main gates, ripping a few holes in the wood and setting it aflame. 'Everyone in the truck!' Salvador cried, getting back to his feet. 'We go in through the front!'

All eighteen men scrambled back aboard the truck, cramping the interior of the main cab and clinging to the sides. Swain got in behind the wheel and revved up the engine, then let up on the clutch and drove at full speed towards what seemed to be the weakest section of the gate. The truck itself weighed more than a few tons, and the added weight of the renegades provided even more force behind the impact, which shattered the burning, bullet-riddled gate into shards of flaming wood.

The feeling of euphoria felt by the desperados was short-lived, because no sooner had the truck ploughed through the gateway and into the courtyard, then it plunged down a sudden incline into a thick pool of soft tar that had been concealed from view by a think layer of dirt and sawdust. The tar grabbed hold of the truck as if it were a dinosaur bound for antiquity, and even when Swain floored the accelerator the vehicle went nowhere but further down into the hole that had been dug and filled with the tar only a few short hours before.

By this time Hannibal had jockeyed his swivel chair around from the back of the mission to a point where he had a clear view of the thugs' predicament from atop the orphange. Beside him, Murdock had loaded up his firing squad and adjusted the beam so that his guns were aimed at the truck. BA and Peck flanked the disabled vehicle on either side, each man armed with an M-16. Amy had retreated behind the trash dumpster, but she was still within throwing range of the truck.

'Give it up!' Hannibal shouted to Salvador. 'Tell your men to throw their weapons past the tar pits!'

One of the reinforcements decided to attempt escape, and he lunged away from the side of the truck, almost clearing the tar, Almost wasn't good enough, though, and he was mired knee-deep in the black ooze in a matter of seconds.

'Anyone else wanna try their luck?' Peck taunted.

Somebody else took a potshot at Peck, and Hannibal promptly fired a shot into the man's forearm, forcing him off the truck and into the tar.

The desperados needed no further persuasion. One by one, they tossed their weapons aside and waited in brooding silence for the final indignities of capture and imprisonment.

'That's it, guys,' Hannibal called out as he got out of the swivel chair and climbed down a ladder to the courtyard. He stuck his head inside the orphanage long enough to shout that it was safe for the nuns and children to come up from the wine cellar, then strode across the open ground to the tar pit. Addressing the prisoners, he said, 'You've got two choices. You can stay put until the *federales* show up to ship you out of the country, or you can get some more fancy ideas about making a run for it and end up as fossil material in the bottom of the pit. Take your time thinking about it, because you'll be under armed guard until you're out of our hair, one way or another.'

Less than half of the criminals understood English, but they all knew the language spoken by Peck's and B.A.'s M-16's, and they didn't want to risk having to hear the guns raise their voices. They stayed put.

The Mother Superior finally appeared in the doorway of the orphanage and stared out at the limited destruction that had led to the capture of her tormentors.

'Well, Mother Superior,' Hannibal said, noting her look of thinly-veiled astonishment. 'Not too shabby, huh?'

The nun had to think for some time before she could express herself in a way that avoided sanctioning the means by which the mission had been rid of its renegades. 'The Lord has indeed been with us,' she finally conceded.

'That may be true, but *I* came up with the plan to capture these guys,' Hannibal reminded her.

'Through the Lord's divine guidance,' the nun clarified. 'He saw to it that we had the tar, after all.'

'I won't argue with you, ma'am,' Hannibal said. 'The point is, now you can go back to doing what you're best at without being forced to live in terror on account of some half-drunken thugs.'

The Mother Superior took in the motley throng filling the courtyard, trying to distinguish between the A-Team and the cutthroats they'd apprehended. She then shrugged her shoulders and turned to go back inside. Once she was in the doorway, however, she stopped and looked back at Hannibal once more. 'Thank you,' she said simply.

Hannibal nodded and gave the nun a wide grin. 'You're welcome.'

THIRTY-THREE

When the *federales* arrived at the rear entrance to Santa Maria's in response to an anonymous phone tip, they found Salvador and his men bound and gagged in a tight circle outside the gates, ready to be transferred into a truck and carted away. The officer in charge of the apprehension asked the Mother Superior how the men had come to be captured, but the nun was vague in answering, referring to the age-old axiom that 'The Lord sometimes works in mysterious ways'. The A-Team, unwilling to draw attention to their own outlaw status, were content to remain in the rooftop shadows, where they had kept the prisoners guarded until the arrival of the local authorities. Once Salvador's gang had been taken away, the Americans descended from the rooftops and were treated to the most sumptuous supper that could be arranged with the mission's food supply. Following the festivities, the team wandered off to prepared bunks and fell into a deep, long-due slumber.

The following morning, Amy knocked on the doorframe of the room where Hannibal and Murdock were snoring soundly.

'Day's a-wasting, boys,' she called out cheerfully.

Hannibal and Murdock both groaned as they crawled out of their respective dreams and rejoined the world of the waking. Hannibal was the first to notice that the third bunk in the room was empty. 'Where's BA?' he said with a yawn.

'I don't know,' Amy said. 'When I got up, he was already gone. He took our truck, wherever he went.'

'And where's Face?'

'Out pacing around the courtyard. It's not easy being in love with a nun.'

'I wouldn't know,' Hannibal said as he sat up on his bunk

189

and stretched. Looking across the room, he noticed Murdock retrieving his golfball from underneath his pillow. 'What are you doing, Murdock, trying to recruit a fairy godmother for your Golfball Liberation Army?'

'Just keepin' GB warm,' Murdock replied defensively as he buffed the ball on his shirt before stuffing it back in his pocket. 'He's not used to this climate, after all.'

The rest of the orphanage was quiet, but outside the courtyard was alive with the activity of playing children. Murdock, Amy, and Hannibal went out to see the Mother Superior watching over the children to make sure they didn't stray too close to the tar pit.

'There should be enough salvageable tar to patch the roof, sister,' Hannibal told the nun as they joined her. 'We'd stick around and help, but we've already stayed in one place longer than we can afford to.'

'That's okay, I've arranged to have some men come out and fix things up here,' the Mother Superior said. 'If you'll recall, there was some reward money for the capture of those criminals. I'd just like enough to put things back in order, then you can have the rest.'

'We wouldn't dream of it,' Hannibal said.

The four of them paused a moment to watch the orphans frolic, then the Mother Superior sighed, 'It's good to hear the children laughing. For a time, I thought I'd never hear that sound again.'

'Well, Reverend Mother, I don't think you'll be harbouring fugitives here for a long time,' Hannibal reflected .'Of course, if you do run into trouble again, you know where you can reach us.'

'Well, actually, the story surrounding all of you is rather sketchy...'

'It's kind of a sordid tale,' Murdock confided. 'Not the kind gospels are usually written about.'

'If you'd like to make a full confession,' the nun offered, 'Father Lopez will be here this afternoon...'

'Thanks, Reverend Mother,' Amy said, 'But I don't think we'd want to take up all his time.'

Hannibal looked over the courtyard, but couldn't see

Peck. 'Hey, Amy, I thought you said Face was out here.'

'He just went to the church,' the Mother Superior explained. 'I think Sister Theresa is there praying. They know each other, don't they?'

'Yeah, I guess you could say that,' Hannibal muttered.

A series of backfires drew their attention to the main gateway, where BA was pulling in, now behind the wheel of the old Bel-Air. He pumped his palm against the horn as he drove around the tar pit and pulled up in front of the others, shouting, 'Come on! Let's go! We're gonna be late!'

'Late for what?' Amy asked.

'The boat leaves at two o'clock sharp,' BA said. 'We gotta drive a couple hours just to get there!'

'The boat?' Hannibal questioned.

'Right on, brother!' BA cried out, baring a grin. 'This time, BA Baracus got us our transportation. It cost most of what we got from them bad dudes, but there's some change left over for meals and stuff. Gonna be a nice cruise! None of that flyin' jive this time!'

'You spent all our money for boat tickets?' Murdock gasped. 'Oh man, not only are we gonna take three blessed weeks to get back to the States, but the Golfball Liberation Army's gonna fold without that pledge money.'

'What pledge money, sucker!' BA snarled. 'I ain't donatin' any dough for your damn golfballs, man!'

The Mother Superior excused herself to tend to the chidlren while Murdock and BA continued to debate The Golfball Issue. Amy and Hannibal stood off to the side, watching the argument with detached amusement.

'You know, Amy, a nice ocean cruise might not be all that bad,' Hannibal said. 'I guess I better go get Face. I'd hate for us to... miss the boat... as they say.'

'Ouch,' Amy winced at the pun.

Across the courtyard, Peck quietly stepped into the vestibule of the mission church. Leslie was up in one of the front pews, saying a rosary. When she finished, she genuflected in the aisle, then walked to the back of the church. Spotting Peck, she flashed an awkward smile.

'I hope you put in a good word for me,' he told her.

'I always do,' Leslie said. 'I told you that.'

They stood together for a few silent moments, each of them feeling the unspoken tension that comes when two people who are close are on the verge of parting. Peck finally reached into his pocket and pulled out the small jewellery box containing his fraternity pin. He withdrew the pin and held it out, saying, 'I know it's kind of dumb, but I really wish you'd keep this.'

Leslie took the pin and clasped it tightly in her hand. 'Thank you. I'll always treasure it.'

'You were right, Leslie,' Peck said. 'If you had told me that night all those years ago that you were going to be a nun, I don't think I could have accepted it. Then, I would have had to say goodbye to you . . . and I'm realizing now how much I hate to do that.'

'Then don't say goodbye,' Leslie told him. 'Besides, it's a word that usually means someone is leaving.'

Peck was confused for a moment. 'Someone *is* leaving,' he said. 'Me.'

Leslie's smile became warmer as she shook her head. 'No, Templeton. Not to me To me, you're always here. And you always will be. In my thoughts and in my heart.'

The two of them shared a brief embrace, filled with as much intimacy as could be managed under the circumstances. Then Hannibal's voice sounded behind them, breaking them apart.

'Face . . .'

Peck took a step back from Leslie. 'My commander calls.'

Leslie nodded and remained in the hall as Peck turned to leave. Before he was out the door, though, she called out, 'Templeton . . .'

Peck stopped in the doorway and glanced back.

'God bless you,' Leslie told him.

'Thanks,' Peck said simply, then walked out the door.

Hannibal noticed the torn expression on his partner's face. 'You okay?'

'Yeah,' Peck said, looking away from Hannibal and walking past him. 'Let's go.'

'Right,' Hannibal said. 'We're on our way . . .'